Ousmane Sembene is now best known as a great film director, sometimes described as 'The Father of African Cinema', but before his first films he had been acclaimed for his novels.

This book, his second novel following *Le Docker Noir* (Black Docker), was first published as *Ô Pays, Mon Beau Peuple!* by Amiot-Dumont in Paris in 1957, three years before Senegal's independence. Never previously translated into English, *Ô Pays*, like *Le Docker Noir*, was written while Sembene was living in France and remains largely unknown to the English-speaking world.

The novel is set in Ziguinchor, the main town in Casamance, in what is now southern Senegal cut off from Dakar and the rest of the country by The Gambia enclave. It presents a vivid picture of that moment in history when the colonialist mindset of the French officials and traders had not yet changed and but when African opposition was starting to stir both in West Africa and in metropolitan France. It clearly reflects Sembene's own political experiences and philosophy and anticipates the themes of his later storytelling in film and in print.

The novel arose from Sembene's own experiences of pre-war French West Africa, of the war in Europe, as a French trade union activist, and of the contemporary struggle for African independence from France. The work is a passionate cry for the people of his home country to recognise the reality of the colonial situation and to act to liberate their country in the face of apathy and a sense of powerlessness, religious conservatism, and colonial brutality.

Sembene soon concluded that writing in French – or indeed any language – was not the best way of reaching his desired audience. So he turned enthusiastically to cinema where his impact has been immense.

Oh My Country, My Beautiful People !

OUSMANE
SEMBENE

Oh My Country, My Beautiful People !

A Novel

Translation by Nigel Watt

Books of Africa

Books of Africa Ltd.
16 Overhill Road
London
SE22 0PH
United Kingdom

Copyright © Estate of Ousmane Sembene

First published as *Ô Pays, Mon Beau Peuple!*
© Amiot-Dumont, Paris, 1957

Translation by Nigel Watt © Books of Africa, 2024

First published in English by Books of Africa in 2024

ISBN 978-1-915527-25-7 Hardback

A Cataloguing in Publication record for this
book is available from the British Library

Typeset by Worldview Productions

Printed by Short Run Press, Exeter, United Kingdom

To Odette A. and Ginette C.

"Love cares no more for caste or race than a sleeper cares where he sleeps. I went in search of love and I got lost..."

Acknowledgements

Books of Africa wishes to acknowledge the contributions and assistance of Samba Gadjigo, Moustapha El Hadji Diop, Lynn Taylor, Alain Sembene, Marie Prudhomme, Patrick Corcoran, Nigel Watt, and Keith Shiri in assisting with this project.

Translator's Note

In the text there are a number of African words, usually from the Wolof or Joola languages which are the principle ones spoken in Casamance. I have used Wolof and Joola rather than French spellings and I have avoided using footnotes. These words have been italicised on their first usage in the text and I would encourage you to refer to the glossary at the back of the book as necessary. There are also French and Arabic words in the glossary. Where characters in the novel speak little French I have tried to make this comprehensible. Names have been used without accents, for example Agnes, Desiree. We are grateful for advice we have received from Senegalese advisors but I must be responsible for any errors.

Nigel Watt

PART ONE

Chapter 1

The boat began to move up the river again. The water was heavy and yellowish. On one side stretched a plain covered with reeds, a haven for crocodiles. Visible in the distance was the dark fringe of the forest, a place of many dangers. Birds in their heavy flight were passing in formation over the reeds, brushing them lightly with their wings; storks, after catching many fish, rose steeply into the air. On the right bank which the boat was now approaching the forest thrust itself forward, trees jostling to reach the river in a mad rush. The first trees were leaning greedily over the blue green water, their branches and creepers intertwining in unbelievable confusion, a botanic free-for-all. Felled by the water and manhandled by its furious force, palm trees were lying flat on the river, their rugged trunks providing a shelter for young crocodiles, their leaves like water weed abandoned in the current. The haunting perfume of the flowering creepers was mixed with blasts of the smell of hot oil and steam.

The man took a cigarette from his pocket and lit it

mechanically, not ceasing to contemplate the overwhelming beauty of the vegetation. By his side his companion looked rather lost.

As the boat advanced, the estuary grew wider and the view became more stunning. The big trees were now further from the river. Muddy riverbanks appeared where mangroves formed a long dark green line of equal height with their roots shooting up from the water, festooned with bunches of enormous oysters covered and then again uncovered by the tide. Huge flocks of scoters – and other marsh dwellers – flew off at the sound of the engine, and pelicans half out of the water, disturbed from their idleness, plodded off in line. In the sky fish eagles targeted the shoals of fish moving down the river; with their claws they seized carp and pike which they carried into the air with loud cries of victory. Bands of geese and wild duck streaked across the river; and beneath the mangroves, as though pursued by the steam from the boat, kingfishers kept changing their perch, the flash of their glittering plumage moving from one branch to another.

With his bloodshot brown eyes, the man was gazing intently at nature; the cigarette was burning away between his fingers. Turning then towards the woman he said in a serious voice, "Douanier Rousseau should have seen this. Shame he didn't come here." The tone of his voice had something compelling about it. It was so deep that it seemed to hover for a time in the air.

"True," she replied. Then, saying no more, they went back to their cabin. Suddenly a great cloud obscured the sun and, without warning, rain began to fall with a deafening sound. There was a disorderly tumult in the gangway as the passengers who had been on the deck were rushing there for shelter.

"Go back to your places, you load of idiots!" shouted a white man whom the Blacks had been watching nervously.

He called a steward to explain to his compatriots that they had no right to remain there. The employee obeyed, but nobody wanted to go back into the rain. Then the white man began to beat people furiously with a *chicotte*. He lashed out, venting his rage at being disobeyed. He struck left and right without regard to gender or age. This caused a terrible scramble in the narrow gangway and some people fell to the ground. Suddenly the white man collapsed, struck by a left hook on the chin and then another in the stomach.

Standing in front of him the black man was waiting with his inordinately long arms almost reaching his knees, his fists clenched ready to strike again. The white man who had not yet recovered from his shock rose slowly, staring at the black giant and merely wiped the blood that was pouring out of his mouth from his immaculate cuff. Now face to face they were glaring at each other. Only the woman with her frail arms was holding them apart.

"That's enough, Faye," she begged.

Like two dogs they were looking each other up and down. The Blacks could not believe their eyes. Who was this colossus that broke the taboo? Beat up a white man? Brothers were rotting in prison for less than that. Coming from all sides, the occupants of the cabins were asking: "Are the natives in revolt?"

Fear could be seen on all the black faces. One woman was weeping: her baby's head was bleeding. The rebel, as Faye had been described by the white woman, forced a passage through his people, took the child and handed him to his companion who was following him. "Get him treated by the captain…"

No-one had yet dared to ask him any questions. Since he had embarked the night before in Dakar he had only opened his mouth to eat and to talk very quietly to his companion.

On board he had aroused curiosity as much in the Whites as well as the Blacks because of his silence, and because of this white woman who followed him around like a shadow.

She soon came back with the child in her arms, his head bandaged. "Thank you, madam," said the black woman.

Oumar Faye was from Casamance. He was going back to his paternal home after an absence of eight years having left his native land – as had a number of his friends – to join the war in Europe. He was returning four years after the victory. He had fought his way through North Africa and France and reached Baden-Baden in Germany where he stopped; he was then demobilised and he married a white woman. Wounded twice, he had been decorated with a military medal and the *Croix de Guerre*. Although he hardly ever wore them, he guarded his medals jealously.

Back in their cabin he lay down on the narrow bed with his arms folded under his head. The woman spoke: "Why did you get into a fight again? Did you just want to draw attention to yourself? With them you will never win."

"What would you want? That he should beat them up and I just stand by? Or maybe that I should help him?" He then spoke more softly as if to apologise for the sharpness of his response.

"We'll arrive any minute…is the luggage packed?"

But he was thinking of what the young woman had just said: "You will never win." In Africa the Whites are the masters and if you attack them you are asking to be defeated.

In numerous ways Faye had perfectly assimilated the thought processes of the Whites and how they react, while keeping deep in his heart his people's heritage. He had seen a lot and learned a lot during his years in Europe: his attitudes had been overturned. He had even come to the point of making no excuses for his brothers: their divisions, their tribal prejudices that seemed to make any chance of social progress an illusion, their narrow outlook and the childishness of some of their 'anti-White' reactions.

She was looking at his face with his slightly flat nose and his smooth forehead where a prominent vein buried itself beneath the thick mass of his hair.

Her very white skin contrasted brilliantly with his; her slender body – she was tall – was tightly wrapped in a linen outfit. Now and then she bowed her head as if her hair weighed heavily on her neck. Her eyebrows were clearly defined. She was really no beauty but she had the loveliness of her twenty-two years.

Wherever she went, Isabelle knew what to expect. This was no pleasure trip – but she would be with her husband. What he had taught her about the behaviour and customs of his country, and also what she had read, would enable her to cushion the numerous shocks caused by challenging the beliefs and fanaticism of his family. Besides, she had such confidence in him, boundless confidence! She never held him to account. She just looked after him and occasionally put him right. They lived very much for each other. They were a devoted couple walking along two parallel roads and, for the future, she gave him strength.

When the telegram arrived that day at Fayene, Faye's home at Santhiaba, the news spread rapidly to all the family. Moussa Faye never took a decision lightly. His son and daughter-in-law would not arrive until the next day and he took time to think about it. He was the *imam* at the mosque and was venerated not only for this but also for his age. Five times a day he gave guidance to the faithful. For him everything was in the Koran and it was in this holy book that he found the basis for the decisions and the counsel he gave. He was considered strict, even hard-hearted, but he was well-liked by everyone and his wisdom was often sought by the local court. The presence of his three wives made him even more venerable in the eyes of the believers. Moussa Faye ran his affairs in his own way and there were never any disputes between his wives. They each took turns in the conjugal bed. The first wife, Rokhaya Guéye whose son, Oumar Faye, was her only child was affected more than anyone by the news. Hadn't she already made a promise of marriage for her little one? What should she tell the family? Although she was the first wife, Rokhaya Guéye enjoyed no more privileges than the other two.

The second wife, Aminata, was the mother of two boys and a girl. As for the last wife, Fatou, she had two girls. All three had the same maternal rights over Oumar but only his real mother suffered when she heard about the marriage of her son.

It was Uncle Amadou who lived in the same compound with his two wives, his three boys and his two girls who came to explain the text of the telegram to his brother. Moussa Faye was sitting on a mat with his head bowed. telling his beads. He did not utter a word. All the Faye family waited and said nothing. Moussa put on his slippers and went out to the mosque with his hands clasped behind his back.

The gossips crowded beneath the 'palaver' tree in front of the sacred place. They gathered as the hour of prayer approached. All the usual ones were there. M'boup was the eldest of them. His frail limbs could not carry the weight of his body. He walked bent double supported by an *alpenstock* and helped along by his white-haired brother. Assane Sarr was also there, a veteran fisherman who had come many seasons ago in his *pirogue* from Guet N'dar to spend the dry season here. Then there was Malik Diop, the father of four daughters, who was relying on their dowries so that he could end his days in the tranquillity of old age. Thiam was equally adept at fabricating a hoe as making gold or silver jewellery to be worn on the arms, neck or ankles. Massiré N'gom was unequalled in his knowledge of the roots of trees and went so far as to compare himself to a *toubaab* doctor. Finally Samba Raba, the weaver with his loom, never stopped working while joining in the chat. The squeaking of the wooden loom which he never oiled enticed the women to have a look at his bright, varied strips of material. All the leading believers were there.

"Have you had a peaceful afternoon?"

"*Jàam rekk*, peace" everyone replied, "and the family?"

"*Jàam*, and your families?"

"In peace," replied those who were seated.

"May peace increase in this holy place," said Moussa as he squatted down.

"Moussa, I wanted to ask you something… about a rumour that's going around," said the weaver, who had stopped his work, "Is it true what I've heard?" He suddenly stopped and the old man replied: "How can I say yes or no if you don't tell me more about it?"

"They say your son is arriving with a white woman tomorrow, *insh'Allah*?"

"It was after the midday prayers that Amadou told me … Samba, excuse me but I want to know something else. From sunrise to sunset you sit at your loom, leaving it only when nature calls but from west to east and from south to north you know everything that is going on. How do you explain that?"

"The snake has no legs but God makes him walk."

"You can surprise me … but you can't surprise God."

"What will be will be," Demba M'boup remarked philosophically, "The sons of today are not sons any more …"

Then, changing the subject: "Where are they going to stay?"

"At his father's place," responded Massiré, "The son has nowhere but his father's house to go."

"In the time of my late father I never had the courage to wear trousers. Ah, the world is going crazy!"

"What you say is true, M'boup," the craftsman interrupted. "In Dakar the young men and girls go out every night dancing. I wonder how far this corrupt behaviour can go. They imitate the Whites in their debauchery. Drink and disease make them unrecognisable even to their own mothers. And as for the girls, the way they dress reveals every part of their figure…"

"That's true, Samba! The first time I was in Saint-Louis I saw with my own eyes in the Ludo quarter men and women dancing so close together that as an upright person you could be allowed to imagine something else. Ah! May God protect you from such a sight."

"Amen to that."

"What do you expect: if so many young people die it's because they are deserting their ancestral customs, the way of God. And now we are complaining that there is a shortage of water. God is punishing us." As he stopped talking he blew his nose with his fingers and wiped them on the heel of his sandal.

"The toubaabs are angry and are increasing the price of thread."

"Forgive me if I cut you off, son of Guet N'dar," the weaver butted in. He had great pleasure in keeping everyone informed. "What you don't know is that the young people want to expel the white men. They call themselves 'the Reds'. They say that afterwards they will share out everything, that they will abandon the way of God – there will be nothing but eating and making love."

"What Moussa says is true, Samba. You never leave this place and yet you know everything. I'm the oldest among you all and yet I have never heard that. Do you turn into a hyena at night or what? Where do you go every night?"

The weaver had the reputation of knowing everything in advance and many people feared him, for it was said that he was one of those who changed into a wild animal and roamed the bush at night. Having answered all the questions he would often touch his nose and say: "As long as your nose is on your face you will say that I am right." Then he went on with his work.

Looking up at the sky, Moussa said: "I think it's time for prayers." From the only pocket in his *boubou* the doyen took out a watch and said: "We still have a little time."

Then Massiré started: "I was in the war of 1914-18. Moussa was there. He came and joined me in 1915. I remember it as clearly as the couscous I ate yesterday evening. Blaise Diagne came and shook my hand, for I was a corporal. Then he called us together and said that the king of *Tugal* counted on us to drive out the Allemands (Germans). I won't tell you anything about Verdun, or the Dardanelles or Salonika. That's where thousands of soldiers died. I lost an uncle and a brother. That's also where I was gassed – and I've still some gas in my body. I've never seen so many corpses. Despite the cold we mounted the attack using our machetes. The white soldiers repeated *laqad jaakum* after us. After this I was decorated by the colonel…. Yes, my medals, I won them and in fact it was there that I was presented with this baton," he said as he displayed his stick… "and I admit I had relations with toubaab women. A man is a man wherever he is in the world, but, honest truth, it never came into my head to marry one of them or to bring her here…"

"One thing. I know you are telling the truth, brother, but in the time of the *Damels* in M'boula Saloum where I was born, each man who set off for battle promised to bring back a slave. We must recognise that the blood of the Fayes flows in Oumar's body."

"You're a *griot*, Massiré," said the old man angrily. "You should be the last to speak and the first to shut up."

"I am the griot of God!"

The imam spoke. "God forgive us, the time has come."

Massiré was at the door of the wooden mosque. He held his hands to his mouth in the form of a loudspeaker and called all the faithful to worship. His solemn voice resounded far and wide. Passers-by turned back to hear more clearly. If they did not understand the Arabic words they knew why the voice was calling, lively and melodious, touching their hearts more deeply than if it was mechanical and automatic.

Straightaway they went in all directions to search for a kettle or a pot for their sacred ablutions. This meant purifying the extremities of their bodies. For them life is nothing; only acts of worship have value; their existence is just a bridge between birth and death. A road with no fork in it. After genuflecting they will wait for the final prayer. That will be when the evening starts to smile, when the stars appear. And then, quietly and carefree, they go their ways after wishing each other a restful night.

The *muezzin* sounding through Fayene tore Rokhaya away from her lamentations. Worship was compulsory for everyone. Soon the women would emerge from all sides and line up behind the men. Then it was the turn of the little ones and as the women guided them they repeated the same verses of the Koran that their husbands were chanting only a short distance away. Selflessly, they submitted to the rite of worship. They bowed down then rose again, sitting down on the ground gracefully in perfect unison, their heads covered with a *tiavali*. There was something very pure in the atmosphere that evening. They were like those wives of nomads in the middle of the desert who are surprised when the hour of prayer strikes and who are only conscious of it for a minute. When the prayers ended heads were turning left to right and from right to left, forefingers were pointing up and down, lips were opening and closing to the sound of chatter and then the ebony rosary appeared encrusted with silver thread or beads of coral that seemed to murmur softly as it slipped between their fingers.

The night descended as though it were enchanted. In the half-light the crowd at prayer could only be distinguished by the colour of their wrappers. Finally, every woman arrived home but before setting off, each one touched her forefinger to her face, and they all joined hands as a gesture of sisterly love of God.

Back at Fayene, right in the middle of the central room, men and women were seated around the family meal, digging in with their hands. It was the evening meal of soup. A blind man standing at the threshold of the door was begging in a piercing voice.

"God's creation, give us your *m'balou*." said the imam. The cripple, leaning on his stick, felt his way guided by his acute hearing. He held out a receptacle which was duly filled.

"May God provide you with a dwelling place, may his infinite goodness lead you into His paradise and guide you in this lowly world ... May the Holy Prophet take you into his blessed protection. May evil pursue your enemies. May

Allah preserve you from temptation."

Everyone responded: "Amen, amen," while he continued to recite: "May God give you long life, that you may see your children's children and their grandchildren." "Amen, amen," they went on interminably. Then the beggar went away.

Amadou spoke to his eldest daughter: "Seynabou, tomorrow you will sweep the guest room."

"Your brother is arriving with his wife," added Rokhaya angrily.

"What's done is done. You have no more authority over your son now than I have. We have to understand that if they wanted nothing to do with us they would not have come back."

"It would have been better for him to have died in the war than to do what he has done. If ... if only I had suspected this I would have strangled him with this very hand," she said, taking her hand out of the food to emphasise the point.

"Remember that the children can hear you," her husband remarked. In response she said as she stood up: "Have a peaceful night!"

Rokhaya did not sleep. Memories of the first years of her marriage passed again and again through her tired head. Her first children had all died at birth. It was said that the evil eye was hounding her. From the start of her new pregnancy, to guard against the child dying she decided to comb the area to find a sorcerer. (In a country where it is forbidden to be sterile, a woman cannot live among her rivals without being rejected. In many cases a divorce is demanded, the dowry repaid and shame inflicted on the family. But it sometimes happens that the woman remarries and gives birth to a child.)

It was on a night like this that Rokhaya gave birth to a boy.

She had wept bitterly, not from sadness but from the doubt she still had in her heart. She had taken all kinds of potions, she was surrounded by charms, horns, amulets and roots to protect her from the evil eye. Eight days after his birth she had pierced a hole in the lobe of his left ear and given him the name Xaar-Yàlla (Waits for God), the name she had given him after her earlier still births. Every Friday for seven years dressed in rags she humiliated herself by begging. Nobody knew why she did this but her wanderings gained sympathy mixed with pity for this mother who simply wanted her son to live, by whatever possible means. The elders gave her plenty of advice about this.

Then the little one had to contend with diseases. When he showed the first symptoms of infantile illness she did not want to see any 'doctor'. This is when she took her first steps to be a sorceress. She would go out at night with her baby on her back and only return at dawn. The only thing she cared about was that her child should live. When the second wife was introduced to the house she felt a sense of relief and she devoted herself more freely to her sorcery. Then came the third wife and this relieved her still more. People said she was slightly crazy, but she had acquired a very thorough knowledge of maternity. She was often consulted about girls' problems; mothers used to come to see her regarding their sons-in-law – and she would help them as best she could. Her rivals had at first been frightened of her. Now they felt protected.

When she and her son were separated he had just turned nineteen. Soldiers were needed in the land of the toubaabs. That day her sadness almost drove her mad. The Friday after the announcement of his departure she shut herself away with him and asked him never to be without the fetishes that she was giving him, reminding him that such and such a piece of wood must be thrown into the sea and this powder must be drunk before he was influenced by anything from Tugal.

Her son departed and during the hostilities he sent news from all the places where he fought on the front. When she got the news that he was wounded it made her ill, weeping as if her Xaar-Yàlla was dead. She even brought out the *oboles*, the alms for a dead person. Some people ended up believing that this news was really true.

Finally at dawn she stopped reminiscing and sleep overcame her. In the morning as the cocks were crowing, the sound of pestles thumping in mortars in every back yard was like a summons to go to work. Seynabou, half-dressed, was pounding millet. In the dim light of dawn her body seemed to merge with the trunk of the mango tree behind her. She was humming to the rhythm of an ancient chant and her soft voice mingled with the tinkle of her bracelets. As the sun appeared over the trees it made her black body glisten and her sweat ran down onto her wrapper. Her breasts, already developed, rose and fell in response to the movement of her shoulders.

"Can I come and sift the flour?" asked her mother who was coming out of the conjugal bedroom. "Wait a bit, you can start making the *kinkilibaa*."

All around the girl the chickens were pecking at the fallen grains, scratching the ground with their feet. Her mother reproached her. "Put on your blouse. Aren't you ashamed, displaying yourself quite naked?" Obediently she put on a blouse with puffed sleeves which reached her elbows. All the family were up and about, asking each other if they had a good night.

"Seynabou Faye … did you sleep well?" came a man's voice. Looking to see where the call came from she stood on tiptoe and over the fence she spotted a white helmet waving. "Diagne! I didn't see you. How did you pass the night?" "Jàmm …and your family?" "Jàmm," she replied. "You never came yesterday. Yet I was waiting for you."

"Oh! I had a lot of work in the office. You know, when I'm away nothing goes right. They send us young guys who don't understand anything about this work … Besides, it seems that your brother is arriving today with a white woman?"

"Who told you that?" asked Seynabou. Pretending to be surprised, she held her thumb under her chin. "I heard Samba Baba say so to Papa Gomis at the shop."

"It's true."

"So what does Daddy Moussa say? Has there been an explosion yet?"

"Nothing. His mother didn't eat anything yesterday evening. I've not yet seen her this morning; she is usually the first to get up…"

"Maybe she's dead."

"Sometimes your mouth is full of filth, Diagne. Are you coming this evening?"

"What are you cooking?"

"Whatever you want."

He felt his male pride flattered. It was true that she never refused him anything … a shame she was so young, he said to himself, for at that age a girl is quick to get pregnant.

"Seynabou! I can't hear you pounding," cried her mother from inside the kitchen. "I'm doing it!" she shouted. Then discreetly to the boy she said, "See you this evening." "Yes, I'll come with my crowd."

Children were yawning as they came out of their houses. Their faces were getting a good wash. Then they were given what was left of the last evening's meal. This was said to 'awaken the spirits'. Then they were setting off for the *daara*. Already the sun was beating down on the zinc roofs, causing a rustling sound, and burning the mud walls.

Everyone was present for the main meal of the day. The imminent arrival of Oumar was on everyone's mind. Up till then the old man had said nothing. Avoiding inquisitive eyes he pondered over the things that had been said. Rokhaya, the mother, had not been seen at all that morning.

"Amadou, you will go and welcome them at the port…. Seynabou, is the bedroom ready?"

"Yes father," she replied, not daring to raise her eyes and holding the bowl with her thumb and forefinger. The father went on: "From now on I don't want anyone to talk to me about them. There's no question of throwing them out of the house. People were saying: 'This is Moussa's son, come home at last!' I'll speak to him …. Otherwise, you tell him, Amadou."

His brother spoke, putting the mouthful of rice he was about to eat back in the bowl, "We should consider carefully before doing whatever has to be done. Your son has grown up. He is a man. He's aware of the consequences of what he has done and if you say something that offends him you will regret it. Hear him first."

"You, you always take his side. When I wanted to send him to Mauritania to learn the Koran you were against it and, because of you, I sent him to school. Now look what we are landed with. How will a white woman live with us? Have you thought about this? Will she know how to pound millet? Will she eat with us from the same bowl? Will she think we are clean or dirty as do those of her race who are only here to exploit us?"

"Don't forget what he was before he left … The war has changed everything."

"I was in the war – and so were you."

"He knows the Koran as you do, and, as for his wife, I know that he has told her all about our way of life even though that has changed. There is a ..."

"The whole world has gone mad", interrupted Aminata

"Woman, we're not asking your opinion."

"I merely said that the world had gone crazy."

Amadou sounded rather irritated: "When men are speaking, a woman who has been taught good manners must keep quiet." He continued: "Right, I will go with young Gomis and find them. We must not make ourselves blind because of his wife, especially since we know nothing about her." Amadou Faye had great respect for his nephew. The meal continued in total silence.

The boat skirted the final stretch of the estuary. The Boudoli quarter could be seen in the distance with its silvery roofs glistening in the weakening light of day. The unequally aligned wharfs seemed to rise out of the water. The steam glided over the flat stretch of water and fishermen vigorously rowed out of the way. The boat's arrival attracted a crowd, all curious. The news had spread like a bush fire fanned by the wind. The whole town was there, – 'from bosses to servants' as they say. The quay throbbed with feverish excitement, bursts of laughter, exclamations in different languages, lengthy greetings and loud voices wanting to know the latest news. In the crowd could be seen Joola women carrying demijohns of palm wine on their heads with an extraordinary sense of balance; beautiful girls nonchalantly rubbing their teeth; brightly coloured clothing; naked torsos; extremely white suits; and boubous like sails inflated by the wind.

Once the formalities were completed people were allowed to disembark.

"Perhaps nobody's come to look for us? Don't forget your sun hat," Oumar advised his wife. Suddenly she said, "Oh, I'm frightened."

"Me too, although I'm returning home. Come on, we must control ourselves, otherwise we will fail." He added somewhat ironically, "Anyway, it would be pretty difficult to turn back."

He too was fearful and a cold feeling flowed through his veins and made the palms of his hands sticky with sweat. "Are you ready?"

"Wait while I look through the porthole ... wow, what a crowd of people!"

"My father isn't there. I knew that already."

Taking his courage in his hands he went out and found himself face to face with his antagonist of that morning. They looked at each other and the white man did not hide his resentment. This look of such hatred nearly made Faye attack him again but Isabelle, suddenly appearing from the cabin, led him away.

They reached the gangway. For a moment he eyed the crowd as though unconcerned. As for Isabelle, she felt that she had been stripped bare by these staring eyes. She nearly lost her balance but he, lithe as a young animal, held her arm. She would have preferred going through fire rather than having so many people looking at her, greedy with curiosity. With Oumar still supporting her they went down the gangway. As they touched dry land the wall of onlookers opened and closed as they passed. Suddenly they saw Amadou waiting for them, with a rather inscrutable expression and accompanied by a young man who seemed to be the same age as Faye.

"Isabelle, this is my uncle." She took out a handkerchief and wiped her face. The two men shook hands. Oumar introduced his wife then, turning towards the other one and recognising him they threw their arms around each other.

"Gomis, I thought you were in Dakar! Let me introduce my wife ..."

"Madame, I'm happy to be among the first to meet you on African soil," he said, bowing respectfully.

"Thank you," she replied.

Amadou, speaking Wolof, said it was time to go.

"Is this yours, this old banger? Do you think that with all our stuff ...?"

"Get in. We shall soon see."

On the tarmac road the vehicle moved easily. It stopped on the main square to allow the old man to get off and again he shook hands with Isabelle. Then it was just the three of them again.

"Tell me, how are things going, my friend?"

"Not brilliantly. You're not planning to run a transport business are you?"

"No ... no such thing. I've something else in mind."

"I heard on the quay that you beat up the manager of Cosono (a shipping company) ..."

Isabelle was sitting still between the two men.

Gomis continued: "You didn't do enough. You should have thrown him overboard. He's the biggest bastard in the country... excuse my language, Madame. In his shop he beats everybody. In the street he forces everyone to salute him."

"Where does he come from?"

"From Upper Volta (Burkina Faso)."

"And how long has he been here?"

"About two years."

"What do the old folk say about him?"

"They don't care since nobody bothers them."

"What about you, the young people?"

"Us, we're powerless to do anything either…"

Faye suddenly interrupted in a broken voice: "My dear, we have arrived." They had hardly touched the ground when a swarm of kids from the neighbourhood surrounded them. Forcing a passage through the crowd with great difficulty, they held hands as they entered Fayene. Waiting for them was Rokhaya, standing in the middle of the house.

"I'll eat my hat if she hasn't been up to some witchcraft … I left her eight years ago at this same spot and she is still there, but there's nothing to fear."

"That's easily said …"

"Stop it, Isabelle."

The mother and the son were eying each other. Tears were streaming down the old woman's face. She was heartbroken to see her boy holding hands with a white woman. Who was she, this woman? Why had she followed her son all the way here? Had she snatched away the love that her Xaar owed her? Didn't she know that she, Rokhaya, never had anything to do with white people? So what was a white woman doing with her little boy? Did the land of the toubaabs lack men so that their daughters began marrying Blacks? What sickness drove Xaar to marry such a person? Were black girls no longer to his taste? Were they not pretty enough? So many questions poured into her mind, jostled with each other and tore her apart! Standing there she felt the sadness that only women who have given birth can feel. She looked closely at the white creature. For her, Isabelle was not a woman at all.

Isabelle did not exactly know if the drama taking place between mother and son was really about her. Finally Rokhaya threw herself into Faye's arms, sobbing: "It's my little one, my very own, my Xaar-Yàlla."

"Don't cry, Mother… I'm not dead."

As though enslaved by the man the woman's wrinkled palm caressed the face which for her was still that of a child.

"You are still young, with no beard…. Oh, my son you must be feeling tired!"

"Mother, I am not here on my own." The joy of seeing him again had made her forget her bitter disappointment. She bit her lip. Isabelle had come back beside her husband.

"Bonzour Madame," said Rokhaya, shaking her daughter-in-law's hand. "Bonjour Maman," Isabelle replied.

Rokhaya held the white hand in hers, then beckoned her into a neighbouring room. Despite her disapproval, she experienced a true feeling of being a woman and a mother. The only things that drove her were her maternal rights, the love of a mother who sees in the fruit of her body a part of herself which she must protect and would always be ready to defend. She searched for the words, then said: "Beaucoup solie, Madame, papa, mama, France…"

"Oui," whispered the young woman.

"France. Long way. You tired? Sleep?" She pointed to an iron bedstead. She spoke while shaking her head and her piercing look caused Isabelle to look down. Although the words of her mother-in-law were in no way worrying she was none-theless fearful. And the fact that she could only understand about half of what Rokhaya was saying discouraged her even more. She looked surreptitiously at the old woman whose neckerchief was tied behind her head revealing a few locks of grey hair.

Faye called: "*Yaay*".

"*Kaay*", the old woman replied.

"I didn't know I was disturbing a tête-à-tête," said Oumar as he came to join them. He added: "My mother says you are beautiful and she hopes you will be a good wife. Now you must come with me so I can introduce you to all the

Faye family. The others have the same rights over us both, including my uncle's two wives."

"I hope you're not going to imitate your father and your uncle."

"Don't say that."

"Swine!"

"If I explained that to my mother!" he laughed. "Women here must not lack respect for their lord and master." He tickled her chin. She said: "That doesn't matter, but three wives for one man, that's too many. I will never understand it…"

"You talk too much, and much too much to think properly," he said philosophically.

This is how Isabelle got to know her second family.

Already the setting sun seemed lost among the foliage of the huge trees. The room which they had been offered was nothing special: an old metal bed, a wooden chair and walls painted white. However, Oumar had something on his mind. "I believe my father does not want to receive us and that upsets me," he explained.

"We're both upset but the moment I'm with you, the main thing…"

"You just rest," he said. "I'm going to see the neighbours." And off he went to make the calls that African courtesy demanded of someone who had made a long journey.

Nothing had changed. The same maze of footpaths, the straw huts still about to collapse, the piles of rubbish; the whole life of a crowded community was there. Children were playing in the clearings. Oumar could not recognise them: some had grown up, others had been born. He encountered girls who when he left were just starting to join the ranks of women but today were mothers and totally unrecognisable. People who were curious to see his 'other half' invited him to visit them. He replied, promising to introduce his wife to them.

The most awkward visit was to the family of his 'betrothed'. Knowing his mother's intentions he wanted to turn back but the kids had spotted him and they came to face him. It was the mother who received and introduced him: "Aida," she called, "come and greet your husband."

A girl with a timid expression approached and knelt down at Oumar's feet. She had very dark skin and very large eyes. He quickly told her to stand up. "I've come simply to greet you."

"It's very good of you. How is your wife doing?" asked the mother.

"Fine," he replied.

An interminable conversation ensued which upset him even more since he had come to break the former promise made to the daughter. He made up his mind. "I am asking both of you to forgive me, but I cannot marry Aida."

The mother replied sharply: "You don't mince words, do you? Is that what you learnt in the land of the toubaabs? You should know that not every branch is for the birds to rest on. But maybe you want to return to where you just came from?" Safiétou, the mother, had the reputation of always speaking with a double meaning and this really annoyed Faye.

"I said nothing of the sort. I came out of respect to withdraw from the promise made by my mother, and as for your second point what counts is not the colour of the cloth but its strength. I'm leaving now. Greetings to Papa Souleymane."

The girl accompanied him to the door. "Xaar," she said, "Don't be angry. My mother did not want to annoy you. You simply misunderstood each other."

On his return Oumar told Rokhaya all about the conversation. She promised to sort things out. They went to bed early that night.

Chapter 2

The main square was situated between the small market and the Santhiaba quarter. It formed a huge quadrilateral from which small streets branched out in all directions. Mango and mahogany trees provided shade and there was a huge kapok tree whose roots looked like the bodies of sleeping children. It was on this square that the elder Gomis had settled and started a family. His shop was the place to go for everything you needed: candles, paraffin, raw tobacco, snuff, cloth, cheap jewellery …. The shop was also a meeting place for young people. When the weather was good benches were put out and at the end of the day people came and sat outside his door under the trees.

"Bonjour, Papa Gomis…hasn't Jean come yet?" asked one as he arrived.

"No, doctor, but he won't be long I'm sure. He just came by with Faye."

"Could you tell me if he's going to Boucot this evening?"

"Not as far as I know, son," replied the shopkeeper. The doctor sat down and opened his newspaper. He was about thirty-two to thirty-five years old. He had two small tribal scars on his cheeks. His ponderous speech and his drawl indicated that he was not from this region. He was born in Dahomey (Benin) which was known as the 'Latin Quarter' of French West Africa.

"Hi Agbo," said a new arrival with a casual gesture as he

was inching his way through the shop.

"Good evening, Diagne," Gomis replied without looking up from his newspaper.

Then Diagne sat down beside him and within a few minutes a large number of young men had gathered. There was M'boup, who worked at Cosono, the shipping company, dressed African style in a local indigo dyed kaftan, with his beret under his arm. Dieng, an agent working for the same company, was dressed in a similar outfit. Seck, the teacher, was obliged by his headmaster to dress in the European style. And there were still others.

"Dieng, are you coming with me this evening?" asked Diagne.

"No, I've got work at the Fayes' house."

"Why don't you just say you're scared of the old man?"

Agbo the doctor intervened: "I'd never understand Diagne in a hundred years! You've relations with all the girls at the same time, one night with one and tomorrow with another. How can you manage that with what you earn?"

"Tell me to pay you, for – it's true – I owe you some money, but spare me your morals..."

"But no, no ... understand what I'm saying."

"You're incapable of doing like me, do you admit it?"

"Ah! On that we agree!"

"That's enough, you two. They say there's not a single day when you're not squabbling," said the teacher who made himself obeyed here just as effectively as in the classroom.

Suddenly Gomis' son's vehicle drew up in a cloud of dust and stopped at the door of the shop.

"How is Faye getting on?"

"Very well, Mr Seck," Jean Gomis replied, making fun of him.

"Is she good looking, his wife?" asked M'boup. "Say,

does she speak Joola or Portuguese?"

They all began to laugh at the question.

"She's well built, tall, with black silky hair, a pleasant voice … and unfortunately she only speaks French, perhaps Latin. Do you speak Latin?"

"Oh," he joked, with appropriate gestures, "that's the language jabbered by crocodiles!"

"What gave him the idea of bringing her here?" asked Diagne, shrugging his shoulders. "To Dakar – or to Saint-Louis if he had to … His father is not pleased. This morning I saw Seyna … Me, I wouldn't do anything so stupid."

"Getting married, Diagne, is not stupid."

"Me, with a white woman! Not for all the gold in the world. No way. We would not be able to get along."

"I agree with you. A black man cannot live with a white woman … especially given what her compatriots do in the bush during the harvest season. Now before our very eyes one of us wants to land a 'toubabess' on us. It's way out of the question. He's a traitor, that's all," the shipping agent ended.

Someone in the group interjected: "It appears that he tickled your boss on the boat."

"The only thing I regret is that he didn't chuck him into the water."

"I know Oumar," interrupted Diagne. "He has no school certificate. The only thing he knows about is fishing. And because he has a *brancou* you suddenly want to take him for a hero. In Europe you can find women like that on every street corner. They're just innocent kids. Ask those who've been in the war…"

The shopkeeper's son responded: "What you say is bad, Diagne. You know more than we do, but when you speak about someone you become rude and envious …. Can you

36

tell us something about why they expelled Oumar from school? I'm going to tell you anyway. Someone had stolen a book and no-one knew who it was. After searching in vain for several days they punished the most troublesome kids in the hope of finding the culprit. Since Oumar knew he was innocent he refused to be punished. Then the headmaster started slapping his face. I don't need to tell you that he was given a bloody nose by Faye and that Faye was expelled from school. But that was not the end of it. The boy who had stolen the book was called Dominic and when Oumar learnt who it was he was given something he would not forget. Despite the elders' intervention, Faye refused to go back to the classroom, saying that he was a fisherman and, like his father, nothing but a fisherman. He had always taken weak ones under his wing. They nicknamed him 'Faye the Great'."

"Diagne, you visit his sister. Better look out!"

"Me," he reacted, "You're crazy! He can go to hell and his wife too! So, according to you we should all abandon our traditional way of life?"

"You're mixing everything up," said the doctor. "Assimilating progress doesn't mean renouncing the past. But there are some things we should not do. I personally would not want to marry an illiterate woman."

"A girl's place is in the home," proclaimed Diagne, positioning himself in front of his audience so as to convince them more effectively. "As soon as they started being educated our role is diminished. My daughter will not go to school. To learn what? That our ancestors were the Gauls. We know that they were blond with blue eyes and that she looks like a sack of charcoal .... No, they teach nonsense."

Everyone doubled up with laughter at what this descendant of the Moors was saying, for Diagne's father was from Mauritania and his mother from Saint-Louis. He was a fluent speaker, but for him only one thing mattered: the girls he pursued and on whom he would spend his monthly salary.

The shopkeeper came to the entrance of the shop and remarked: "We are sending our girls to school in any case."

"That's because of your religion."

"Don't confuse education with religion. Anyway, the only difference is that you people are allowed to have several wives."

"The bad thing is that they can now vote! But while we wait for a law to be passed to stop this – which will never happen – I would like to have ten of them!"

"I hear you. Life's nothing without them. But have you just once wondered if they would like to have rivals? What would you say if when you get up in the morning your wife tells you: "Tonight it's my second husband's turn.""

The doctor kept quiet and the laughter grew louder again.

"Yes, it would be funny," Diagne responded, "but it won't happen as long as men keep their eyes focused on the east. Polygamy is the best way of life."

"What about the quarrels between half-brothers, issues of inheritance, the mutual jealousy of women, the absence of love for the man and all the other problems....?"

Then, changing the subject, the doctor asked again: "Jean, are you going to Boucot?"

"I've no petrol left. I've just done two trips for Faye. You can't imagine how much luggage he had."

"He's a toubaab, isn't he?"

"Don't start on that again, Diagne!"

"Okay I'll shut up. Anyway I'm inviting all of you this evening."

"Where?"

"To Fayene."

"I'm coming," said Seck. "But afterwards we'll go to Aida's place."

"Ay, ay ay," Diagne lamented, shaking his arms as if he was walking on burning embers, "her mother doesn't want to see me anymore."

"Not surprising. You've behaved badly to her…"

"What do you mean? I send her a money order each month, have done for eight months. And not once have I managed to have the girl. One day I gave her my *sabador* to wash and what did this old madam say but, 'Give me the price of the soap!' …'Bollocks,' I said to her."

Abdoulaye Diagne was the life and soul of the group. He made fun of everything. He said he liked to enjoy life and when he invited his friends to different homes he aimed to keep up his reputation as a womaniser.

"And you're not polite either," Seck remarked.

"I don't care. It's time for some food. I'm going to take M'boup and anyone who wants to come at eight o'clock."

"Okay," replied M'boup.

As soon as they had departed the conversation suddenly ceased. Calm returned again. Then they got up and departed one by one.

All they really wanted was to live without worrying about the next day. But as the country was waking up from its lethargy, it drove them along like a river carrying away its silt. Their future and that of the people required more from them every day. They aspired to an Africa where they were not living in the middle of a drama where two races were colliding.

Night was falling. Darkness was nibbling away everything visible; then, all of a sudden, the night devoured everything.

Early the next morning Faye had already made a tour of the house. When he returned to the bedroom Isabelle was sitting on the bed.

"Awake already?"

"I slept so well!" she said as she stretched, "I didn't hear you come in last night."

Seynabou served them with coffee and rolls, bought from the only bakery in the town. Then they went out, going towards the bush. Upstream there was nothing to see but coconut palms and toddy palms. On the road to Adeane the sun was burning the leaves on the tallest branches.

They soaked their feet in the warm water of a rivulet.

"You know, I wouldn't mind having a swim," said Isabelle.

"Ahead beside the cemetery there's a marvellous place to bathe."

They cheerfully went there and in fact the stream seemed much wider and cleaner. A half-sloping tree trunk served as a diving board. Water lilies covered the surface of the water, and shrubs gave this improvised swimming pool a feeling of intimacy; the somnolent frogfishes fled in surprise. Without a care for the passage of time the two laughed as they dived, totally naked, again and again into the clear water.

At midday she said, "I'm beginning to feel hungry."

"Damn it, it's so good here."

"Not a sound."

"No cars."

"No metro."

"No newspapers."

"No cinema."

"Ta, ta, ta, you're hooked. It's a deal! Do you like the place?"

"But …, you're not thinking of building a house here?"

"Indeed I am!"

"Oh," she threw herself into his arms, and they toppled together into the water.

"Now let's go home…"

"Can we view the plot of land?"

"Dope, you've been treading the ground of your future abode for a quarter of an hour!"

"Shall we come back here this afternoon?"

"If you like … the house has to be built before the rains start."

"Within three months?"

When they got back to Fayene the place was crowded with people begging, an old custom, for their 'share from the journey'. The aged Rokhaya had invited them to sit down. Oumar, with the haughty dignity of an English lord, greeted them as he passed by and went to shut himself in his room. His mother came to explain to him what the visitors wanted.

"But I've nothing to give them," cried Oumar. "How can you know whether I have any money or not?"

She angrily replied: "If you give them nothing then I'll do so myself."

She was about to leave when Isabelle, who had overheard, courageously handed over a few banknotes.

Faye sulked. "You're an idiot to do that. If you give them money they'll see you as the good girl; if not they will talk ill of you …"

"I'm not doing it out of the goodness of my heart you know, but just to please your mother …. Perhaps she'll say …."

"She can say what she likes," he screamed angrily.

Outside the house a general "Hurrah!" could be heard. All those asking for money wanted to shake hands with Faye. Rokhaya came back and said to Isabelle, "Thank you very much, madam."

Then they spoke in their local language: "Mother, I don't want to give anything, and what's more, she won't give anything more because we have nothing to give."

Rokhaya replied, "But me I'm going to give since I'm not a toubaab."

"It's not a question of being a toubaab or not. Sit down, I'm going to speak frankly to you."

They took their place on the bed and Isabelle sat on the chair, made of tara wood.

"They see me as a good son," Faye began, "because I donate. Imagine for once that I am in need of money and stop giving, what will they say? They will say, 'Look at Oumar Faye who considers himself to be a toubaab, he's a rascal, a bad guy.' They would then see me as a bad son whereas you will always be my mother. Please understand that there are things that shouldn't happen, things that encourage these people's idleness …"

"In a way you talk sense, but these are our customs and I can't do anything else. Even if I had to sell my last *pagne* to satisfy them I would do it."

"Once and for all, I just wanted you to know …" said Faye, but Rokhaya interrupted, her fingers on her lips.

"Don't speak of evil."

Isabelle asked: "What are you talking about?"

"Him…much…mechan," said Rokhaya as she went out.

Oumar took out a cigarette, lit it and, after a few puffs, handed it to his wife.

Then they began to unpack things from a trunk, which they distributed to members of the family – fabric, jewellery, shoes for adults and children, trinkets. All the inhabitants of Fayene lined up to show their gratitude to Isabelle. Her mother-in-law was moved greatly by the gift of a Tyrolean pipe.

To honour the occasion Seynabou served their meal and they ate alone at a table she had prepared in their room. Just as they sat down Amadou arrived. After wishing them bon appétit he spoke to Isabelle in French: "Thank you for presents ... my family too ... much sincere." These words came straight from the heart and Isabelle did not know how to respond; and he, unable to find the words in French, said nothing more. He left the room.

In the afternoon they went again to the same stream to play around like children. No-one saw them return until late in the evening.

"Where were you?" asked his mother anxiously. "Your father wants to see you. He is in the prayer room."

The old man was sitting on an animal skin with his head and his thin neck poking out from the whiteness of his enormous boubou. He did not look up even when his son squatted down near him. He held a string of beads between his fingers and his lips opened and closed as the beads fell to the ground one by one, tac, tac, tac. When the litany was over he took the whole rosary in his hands, blew on it, passed it over his head and said in Arabic: "God is great, Allah akbar, Mohammed is his prophet. Grant us clemency, mercy and His forgiveness in this world and in the next. Guide our spirits as a child guides a blind man ..." Then he turned round to face his son.

Oumar shook the hand that was held out to him.

"How are you, my son?"

"I'm fine. Jaam rek, father."

"Thanks be to God you have returned safe and sound.... This afternoon I looked everywhere for you."

"I was by the stream."

All the time he was conversing with his father, Faye kept his head bowed and he played with his fingers as he did as a little boy. Moussa observed him to see if he had changed very much. Oumar looked at the ground. An African notices a youth's education by the boldness or the humility of his attitude. (Politeness in Africa would be considered as timidity in Europe.)

The silence grew heavier.

"Did you know that your grandmother died in Dakar?"

"Yes. Uncle wrote to me."

If only he could have left his father and postponed this meeting till the next day! It was a tough ordeal for both of them since both knew that only one subject really mattered to them.

Moussa, taken off guard by his son's silence, asked: "What happened between you and this white man?"

Faye told him all about the brawl on the boat. "All day long I've waited to hear about this," Moussa continued. "The administrator called for me because of you; he wanted to see you. Don't you know that kneeling does not hurt your kneecaps? Watch out for him, he is a bad man."

Oumar humbly replied: "Yes, father."

Seeing Oumar's submission, Moussa went on the attack: "By the way, did you think of your mother the day you got married?"

"Yes, a great deal!"

"And what did your conscience tell you?"

Oumar kept quiet. Moussa seized the moment to go deeper: "You are now a man, flying with your own wings …. My daughter will never marry a white man. Do you think you've done the right thing? Tell me? How are you going to live here? Will you eat maize meal? Will your wife draw the water? Will she pound millet or will you do it for her?

In the days to come you won't be able to dine at my place: there's only one kitchen and we eat from the same *gueule*. If she doesn't look down on us will she dip her white hand into it?"

These last words were spoken in a tone of irony which stung Oumar. Each word was like the lash of a whip. He took his punishment without flinching. His father went on ferociously: "You don't know the use of buttocks until the moment you sit down. Think about it, my son."

Oumar clenched his fists and looked his father in the eye and replied: "I am only asking you to help me. I am going to build myself a house …. No, don't worry. Not here, but up among the palm trees. You built this house and I was born here. For my wife and for me I want it to be the same. Everything you have just said to me I have said to myself a hundred times and my wife is equally aware of it…. It's better to get to know each other than to learn about our weaknesses from other people. But I thought that, coming here, I would find a father who would understand me and not a father who would throw me out into the street. Someone else could have accommodated me but in that case what would you have said? 'This is my son who disowns me.' If I had married a Joola it would be the same. The woman I have married is just like any other: she has a father and a mother…. I'm determined to live here in spite of everything …"

Oumar too had a feeling of relief. Now he had begun he would go through with it to the end. He found it very unpleasant confronting his father but, biting his lips, he continued: "I'm leaving this house tomorrow. I shall be going to the palm grove."

At this moment Amadou turned up. He sat down next to them.

"What's the matter?" his uncle asked.

"Nothing," Oumar replied.

"How do you mean nothing when you have tears running down your cheeks?"

"May I go now, father?"

"No, stay," said Moussa.

He told his brother about Oumar's decision but then he turned to his son saying, "So you don't want to live with us under this roof?"

"Father, that's not it …. I have a wife and it's better for her and for us all if I have my own place."

"So you have no need of anybody?"

"I did not say that either, father."

Again a painful silence ensued. The children's laughter could be heard.

Amadou intervened: "I think Oumar is right, Moussa. A son only has his father's house. We have to thank heaven that he didn't remain in Tugal. You should be proud when your son says to you: 'Father, I want a house!'"

"When a rock falls from heaven nothing can stop it. May God do what He wishes."

Moussa then asked his son to introduce his wife to him. Isabelle was with her mother-in-law and Oumar went to find her. She felt frightened as she approached. Her hand vanished in Moussa's grip. She presented him with a parcel and, invited by her husband, sat down with her legs stretched out. Rokhaya remained outside. Only the glow of her pipe could be seen.

The grim old man spoke: "Thank you. Mother…father… Fransse?"

She nodded her head.

"Happy…here?"

"Yes," she replied.

His father's questions displeased Oumar. He put his

arms on her shoulders to guide her in her response. Moussa continued: "No brothers?"

"One sister," said Isabelle.

"I hope and wish that you will be a good wife. And now you may go," he told his son.

As on the previous night Rokhaya did not sleep a wink. She had heard her Xaar-Yàlla tell his father that he was leaving Fayene. But where would he go? She knew nothing yet. She cursed this white race that was turning her little boy away from what was right. Before dawn she was up, sitting between the scrawny roots of a mango tree with her back leaning on its trunk, smoking tobacco.

That morning Oumar thought he was the first to rise. He went to look for young Gomis and his old jalopy. The young man showered him with questions. Was he moving house? Why? Oumar kept his mouth shut, calmly taking a puff of his cigarette. The arrival of the car and the noise of its engine finally woke the whole household.

Faye gave a tug to his wife's foot which was protruding from the blanket: "Get a move on, we're leaving."

Yawning, Isabelle asked, "Where to?"

"To our new home," he replied as he searched in the trunk for all the items they had left in the room. The two young men, assisted by Isabelle, piled the things up as best they could. The old man, Moussa Faye, came out of his quarters and watched the comings and goings of his son. He stopped for a moment to contemplate. By chance Oumar's and his father's eyes met. They both were defiant. Oumar's jaw was clenched as he stared back at his father. His eyes said: 'I'm never coming back'. The imam understood that his son was confronting him …. He turned his gaze away from Oumar and fixed his attention on the white woman. Isabelle felt afraid. She had a cold feeling down her spine. She remained there, nailed to the spot, holding her suitcase in her hand. Then Oumar pushed her towards the car. She breathed, as though freed from a dangerous grip, and her heart began to beat normally again. Moussa passed beside his son saying nothing and proceeded towards the mosque.

Gomis and Faye finished loading the luggage without saying a word. Once everything was on board, Oumar went to find his mother. She was wrapped in a shabby, coarsely woven cloth. Her feet were bare and her discoloured head-dress was awkwardly perched on top of her hair, leaving a few white wisps to escape. She had been observing him all the time. All her thoughts and the words she wanted to say to him dissolved and stuck in her throat as her son approached. She stared at him as if to convince him to stay, but her tongue was tied. She could no longer taste anything, not even the tobacco that she loved the most. Released from the constraint brought about by her sadness, tears gushed out and flooded her face. She sniffed energetically. Oumar did not like this show of weakness.

Suddenly the old lady stood up and pressed the palms of her hands against the cheeks of her Xaar-Yàala. Her melancholy stare seemed to vanish into the distance. The roughness of her hands said more. A fire inside her was burning. She felt sick, frighteningly sick. Oumar tried to console her but his decision was final and he simply said: "I'm going there. You know it's not far."

Rokhaya's hands moved up and down, stroking her chin and the lobes of her ears. In her mind she had lost her son.

"Why are you doing this to me, my son? Why?"

She was begging for a response. "Oh, mother, it's hard to explain …. I think it's better for all of us."

"Did someone say something to you that you did not want

to hear? Or lacking respect? Or is this what your wife wants? Or what?" she asked again begging him for an answer.

"No, no," he replied.

"Is the house too small? Perhaps I am not worthy of being near your wife? I don't dress nicely? Oh, I'll dress smartly and wash myself well to please you. I'll even wear shoes, as I've heard that in the land of the toubaabs they always wear shoes. I'll serve you at table. I'll be your servant … but don't leave me!"

Now she was holding him by the shoulders. Oumar was acutely uncomfortable and felt an agony that affected him greatly. "Oh. Mother, it's not like that. I'm staying in the town. I'll still be with you."

"I want you to be mine and mine alone. I carried you in my womb. I sacrificed everything for you. When I was walking and felt you moving inside me I stopped. If I was asleep I got up and stayed awake. I was contented to know that you were alright. And when you came into the world I watched over you while you were asleep, a thousand times too happy to sleep myself. Your breathing became my life. I watched you waking up to make sure you were happy as you opened your eyes. It happened that I often wondered when you were sleeping if you were not prey to the evil eye. Constantly I clutched you to my heart. I never tired of pouring out my love for you. I gave more than a thousand women would for one child. I wished and I still wish that you could enjoy things that none of your friends could aspire to. I would grant them to you. But, oh my son, I beg you to stay."

She was tired of standing up. She eased herself down onto a root and crossed her legs. She stuffed tobacco into her pipe and relit it, with her eyes all the time on Oumar. Her eyelids were swollen. She exhaled a large puff of smoke.

Oumar spoke: "Mother, it's getting late. I must go now."

She had closed her eyes but she burst out: "I hate your wife! I hate all your people! I would have no peace as long as they lived here. Every time I looked to the east and the sun appeared there I would have no rest. They have taken you away from me ..."

She came forward close enough to touch Isabelle. She looked at her scornfully, then turned towards her son and told him: "She has made you eat her menstrual blood!"

And, speaking in her own language to the young woman in her blue jeans who did not dare to move, she added: "Where you come from don't girls respect their parents then?... And I'm telling the truth," she concluded, shaking her head.

Oumar muttered, as though to himself: "At times she frightens me."

Isabelle asked her husband: "What did she say?"

"Oh, nothing," he replied, sounding weary and disillusioned.

And he gently directed her into the car which drove off in a cloud of light red dust.

Chapter 3

Over a large area the palm trees had been knocked down and their trunks sawn into pieces to be used as required by Isabelle and Faye. They had employed two Papeles, who were famed throughout Casamance for their expertise in construction. These two were hard at work from dawn to nightfall.

Faye and his wife spent the nights in a tent. For Oumar it was a race with the onset of the rainy season, a real battle with nature. The days passed without him visiting his parents. He was so absorbed in his work that he seemed to have forgotten them. He only went to the market to sell his catch on the way back from his day's fishing. He exchanged insignificant, polite and respectful words with his father. For the father, his son was nothing more than a stranger. As for Rokhaya, she made plans every day to visit her son. Behind their backs gossip and slander spread fast. Moussa, they said, had driven away his son and the old lady wanted nothing to do with her daughter-in-law; Oumar, like a typical youth, had abandoned the family home and this brancou considered her in-laws to be dirty. When they saw Rokhaya coming they pretended to keep their mouths shut, but once she had passed the laughter hit her like arrows of fire. All she had left were her tears.

However, one day she plucked up courage and, fighting back the hatred she felt for her daughter-in-law, she set off to go and see her son. Half way there she met her husband.

"Where are you going?"

Embarrassed, she replied: "To see Xaar."

"Go back to our yard," the old man ordered, and without saying another word he left her there.

She turned back. It was two months since she had seen her son. She sobbed repeatedly; could there not have been something rotten in her womb to cause her son to behave like this?

It was only Uncle Amadou who continued to provide moral support for the young couple. He never failed to give them advice and he took no notice of the gossip. At noon one day when the Papeles were having a rest after a hard morning's work, Oumar was at the far end of their plot battling with a palm trunk which he was dragging, one heave at a time, towards the stream. Isabelle was cooking some fish which she had netted by herself.

Amadou spoke to Isabelle: "Bonsour enfants."

Isabelle lifted her head and pulled up a canvas chair. "Ah, uncle, sit down there."

"House finish? Petit, petit."

"Oh, yes," she muttered. "We have a lot more to do still."

"Peu?" His gestures completed the sentence.

Isabelle understood that he wanted to see his nephew. She wiped her fingers before holding them to her mouth and whistling three times. Then, turning to Amadou, she repeated: "Do sit down then. He'll be here in a moment."

Amadou Faye was touched by Isabelle's behaviour. Something inside him said that this was a courageous woman.

He knew his nephew and his affection for him was sincere. Amadou kept saying to himself that the young man knew very well what he had to do and that he never undertook anything without thinking about it carefully.

Oumar arrived, his torso and his feet bare, dressed only in shorts with a broad brimmed hat on his head.

They shook hands. "Hello uncle," he said. "I'm hungry, wife!" He sat on the ground. They were in front of the tent. Some clothes were drying on a palm branch. Oumar scratched his head as he spoke: "I think we shall have finished in a week or two."

Amadou had a look all around the walls which were built of fresh yellow *banco*. At the side were three piles of zinc sheets for when the rafters of the roof would be ready.

"Did the man from Dimbéring come for the shellfish?" asked Amadou.

"No, I saw him the day before yesterday at the market. I told him to wait for me but I've not been back. There are some branches over the stream that I must cut and I want to deepen it so that it will be possible to navigate up to here in a pirogue."

"Incidentally, why are you not coming to the house anymore? Your father asked me today what was preventing you coming to the mosque?"

"To visit the house, impossible. I'm working day and night. I'm not avoiding you but, as you know, time does not wait. In the evening I'm tired. It sometimes happens that I don't sleep for two nights in a row. If my father doesn't want to talk to me it's not because I don't go to prayers, nor even that I don't go to the house. The only person who is really upset is my mother. As for my beliefs, that is a personal matter."

He took a breath and continued: "With you, I can talk. Listen to me: I am a black man and I'm staying that way. I have respect for our customs and for our respect for God. It's just that I'm not a fanatic. Since my return I hear everyone saying: 'God is good. God is good,' obviously when things are going well. And when everything is going badly: 'It's the will of God.' Should I go and swell the ranks of the credulous? No way."

"You have travelled widely and heard many things, but what you are saying is incomprehensible to me."

Oumar poured out his heart. He knew that his father would quickly be made aware of his words. He went ahead anyway, speaking with a serious voice. "I've seen the Arab countries, the source, apparently, of all faiths. Ten times more depraved than us, yes – they cut your throat. They have no more respect for you than for a chicken. As for the Europeans, they're worse. Believe," Oumar went on, "Believe and be poisoned are two…"

Isabelle had listened attentively to her husband. Amadou on the other hand was confused by what he had just heard. He had not entirely grasped the meaning of the words. He said: "So, if you act honestly, people will know …"

Isabelle Faye interrupted their conversation, putting two plates right on the ground in front of them. The uncle shook his head.

"Are you not eating?" she asked.

"Manger…moi venir. (He meant to say, 'I have already eaten before coming here.') Merci, Madame."

"I would like you to say to your uncle that they have a false image of white people …"

Oumar translated Isabelle's words and she continued: "It's true that we invite people for meals, as is done everywhere. But if they arrive at a mealtime they share with us whatever we have to eat …. So, tell him that I insist that he eat with us. It's fish and there's no wine in the sauce."

Oumar reported all these words to his uncle, who bowed his head liked a child.

"Tell your wife that I have eaten already and that if I was

hungry it would not hesitate to join you. For me she is like my daughter. It's not because she's white, but truly I'm not hungry ... I will support you as long as you are doing the right thing. If the day comes when I'm not happy with you, I will make that clear. But," he ended, "as God is my witness, I have dined already."

"Then have a drink," Oumar advised him.

Isabelle brought some well-sugared lemon juice.

Amadou emptied the glass in one gulp and said: "Bien... good, thank you."

A smile quickly lit up Isabelle's face. From the distance came a sound of an approaching vehicle and, through the trees, Gomis' car appeared.

"You're arriving at the right moment, just in time to eat something before you go," said Oumar as the young man's feet touched the ground.

"Oh well, working for you is slavery. Hi Isabelle."

The driver took a plate and helped himself. The pot was placed in the centre and each one took a mouthful.

The uncle spoke: "I have to go back now. Will you come fishing with me one of these days?"

"Sure. For a long time I've been longing to suggest reviving our old team. Remember how in the old days we used to be the strongest."

"Au revoir Madame," said Amadou. Then in Wolof, "Jàmm, have a peaceful evening."

"You too, uncle."

Amadou departed and Oumar gave Gomis his list of orders.

"I need sacks of cement. I have to put coating on the banco. I don't expect to find cracks in the walls in two years' time. And oh, while I think of it, haven't you forgotten to bring the pipes."

Gomis replied with his mouth full. "No but, damn it, it's hard living with you. You forget nothing! Not a thing! Nothing at all!"

"My husband doesn't approve of forgetting or forgiving," Isabelle commented.

"I'm leaving you to your prattle. Time hasn't got an appointment with me."

"And the coffee is on the fire." But Oumar was not listening to his wife. He was gazing at the sky.

"Well, just look," he said, holding Isabelle in his arms while Gomis watched, "When we first got here the clouds were thicker. In the hot season they move from west to east and when they are all in the east they start to move back, but this time they are loaded with water. If I'm not mistaken, this year we are going to enjoy good rains. And earlier than expected."

Isabelle watched with wonder the clouds in the sky. They were all moving in the same direction. Then suddenly she jumped up. The water she was heating had overboiled and spilt all over the fire. Oumar swallowed a little coffee and went back to his work.

The hot season was coming to an end, but, despite a few light gusts of wind that seemed to come from the waters, it remained hot. It seemed that what had only yesterday been an empty space had been filled up bit by bit. Passers-by stopped and looked at the house. The roof was made of the branches of an African fan palm, covered with zinc sheets which created flashes of metallic light. The local people talked about nothing but 'La Palmeraie', the name which they had given to the house.

The young Fayes' new home was surrounded by screens. Fruit trees drew their life from the humid soil. Across a green lawn a central drive led to five steps up to the veranda which surrounded the ground floor. This consisted of four large rooms, well ventilated by French windows. The floors were covered with animal skins and all around the living room books were arranged on shelves. A small staircase made of palm trunks led to the bedrooms on the upper floor. In their bedroom a very large bed made of varnished wood was hidden beneath a mosquito net. Its window overlooked the stream and in the distance there was a wide view over Casamance.

For Oumar this house was the symbol of his ambition, his desire to have a real home of his own. Holding hands with Isabelle they looked with admiration at their handiwork. Yet what they were gazing at still seemed to be a dream! Suddenly Faye lifted her up and she hung round his neck. They moved towards the house. Still holding his wife in his arms, Faye carried her upstairs to their bedroom where he ceremoniously laid her on the bed. Isabelle drew him towards her. Faye smiled at her.

"Here is your house, darling wife, and here are all the keys ..."

"I wonder," she said, "if I must simply be proud of you or if I must adore you too?"

Faye's voice was solemn: "Your actions must be governed by your heart."

"Do you know what I'm thinking about?"

"No," said Faye.

"Of the hotel room where I gave myself to you for the first time ..."

Oumar leant over her. His breath brushed the face of the young woman. He loved to caress her hair this way.

"If we need to call our memories to mind, then there are some other ones which must be obliterated. Come on, let's go for a swim and this evening, just the two of us, celebrate this event. Get a move on! Into the water," he said as he stood up.

Limpid and crystal clear, the water in the stream revealed its sandy depths where swarms of tiny fishes were swimming in perfect tranquillity. At this time of day the feeling of water on the body was the most delightful experience.

Isabelle was already in the water. "Do people come past this place?" she asked.

"Yes, from the nearby villages ... You'll see them. It's exactly at this time they come to tap palm wine."

And suddenly, prompted by an idea that had just come into his head, he uttered a shrill scream.

"You frightened me," cried Isabelle.

"Listen then," he said, pricking up his ears.

Faye got no response, so he shouted again, "Wow, wow, wow." This time from the depth of the woodland the same shout replied to him.

"Did you hear it?" he exclaimed with satisfaction. "Let's go now."

His dark skin shone beneath the silvery droplets of water. With his athletic build, his bulging muscles and his fine limbs he resembled an ebony carving. He moved with great agility. They arrived at the foot of a palm tree where a man was working, tied by a *candabe*, a belt made of palm branches which enabled him to clamber up the tree. The two men spoke to each other for a moment while Isabelle watched them, still in her swimming costume. Then, a step at a time, the man climbed higher with his feet perpendicular to the ground. In no time he reached the top of the tree, with his machete sending the dead palm leaves flying. He made some holes in the most sensitive parts of the trunk and hung gourds there. Then with skill acquired from long experience he swung round to the other side of the tree.

Isabelle exclaimed, "That's fantastic! If I were in his place I'd die of fright …. There must surely be accidents?"

"That's the risk of the job."

"You have no heart!"

"But you have one for me! … Quick, let's go back to the house." They spent that evening enjoying royally the happiness of married life.

Oumar now frequently went fishing with his uncle. They shared the catch. The younger man would sell some of it and dry the rest. People wondered why he preserved the fish. Oumar developed his plan, wisely waiting. Amadou was not making any profit for himself. And it was a surprise for him to watch Isabelle and Oumar skin and clean the fish together, each armed with a knife. What struck Amadou the most was that this woman, Isabelle, was helping her husband with an enthusiasm that was almost passionate and showed unfailing courage.

The dry season was coming to an end. The distant rumbles of thunder were becoming more frequent. Sometimes, rather than fish the nephew obtained a load of oysters from his uncle. Mangrove roots filled the bottom of the boat. Amadou was thoroughly confused …. Oysters, he wondered, whatever for? Faye paid for his share but that did not explain his behaviour, nor the large quantity of dry shells that he was accumulating. And when Amadou was asked what his nephew was up to, all he could say was: "I assure you, I know nothing about it."

Inquisitive people doubted his word. Amadou swore by all his great gods, by his children and by the head of everyone he cherished that he was not aware of the young man's plans. Faye's discretion increasingly weighed on his conscience. That evening his uncle decided to interrogate him.

A few stars were dimly shining as the pirogue moved towards the setting sun. The oars beat the water with a rhythmic cadence. All along the bank the dull outline of the mangroves stood out in the melancholy half-light of the evening. Uncle and nephew had not said a word to each other since the start. The silence resonated on their eardrums. In the semi-darkness Oumar stopped rowing. He was at the prow of the boat. Then after taking up the net he checked it again, stood up and directed operations. His uncle obeyed, avoiding making any noise with the paddle. He threw the net which opened and then let it close itself in the water and after a few seconds he hauled it on board. Some carp, mullet and some other fish were strewn all over the bottom of the pirogue. They moved off. The day's fishing had been good. Rising above the scenery the moon was now flooding the river with a milky carpet. The screeching of night birds mingled with the gurgles of crocodiles.

"Oumar," began his uncle. Then he stopped for a long time before continuing. "I really wanted to know what you plan to do with this stuff you are drying?"

Oumar did not like being asked such questions. But he was touched by his uncle's calm and his seriousness and especially by his silence before asking the question. He lifted his oar out of the water as he was no longer using the net. Amadou followed suit and the pirogue swayed lazily in the water.

"Hear what I say," said Faye, "I want to be a farmer. Soon it will be the rainy season and the workers will have need of it."

Amadou was more and more amazed.

"Tell me, my nephew, are you taking me for a ride by any chance?"

"No, uncle. It's true."

"You know …. No."

Amadou thought it was excessive to say more about it. He only said, "Let's go downstream and we'll fish with hook and line."

They sailed back up the river. The darkness of the night was punctured by the fires lit by the charcoal burners along the riverbanks; further afield the single eye of the lighthouse was flashing. By this time they were close to the deep trench between the water of the river and that of the sea. The mixing of the two was an amazing sight. Faye took out a cigarette, lit it and stretched out on top of his catch while Amadou was baiting a live fish. They had stopped rowing, allowing the boat to drift.

They had been still a long time when there was a sudden, brutal jerk which nearly knocked them overboard. They found themselves drifting towards the open ocean.

"A small tooth sawfish," cried Amadou.

Oumar grabbed the paddle just in time. The creature changed direction, making for the fresh water. To tire out the shark they let it swim upstream. It was not used to this environment and its strength rapidly diminished but it was still treacherous! Catching such a creature required enormous self-control. The swirl of the water caused Oumar to lose his balance. The shark came back towards them, revealing its monstrous shape.

"Don't let it move underneath us!" said Amadou.

But again the shark failed to overturn them and it dived to the other side. Its progress came to a sudden halt once, and then a second time: the creature was making wild leaps with a raging sound that shattered the quiet of the night. The shark now displayed its maximum strength and it literally charged at the two fishermen. They did everything they could to escape but, whether out of malice or treachery, the creature changed direction and started to pursue them. This went on for several hours. The shark floated for a time, then when they neared it again it began to charge. Amadou fell over. The paddle slipped from Faye's hands and was swallowed up in the river. They drifted gently towards the salt water.

"Hold on to the line so it doesn't escape. My arm hurts."

A whitish glow was appearing on the horizon. The night swallowed up the visible shapes of things one by one.

Isabelle walked up and down in the dim light of the paraffin lamp. She did not know what to do. Read? She did not feel like it. Sleep? That was all she could do. With her hair tied in a ponytail, she was wearing trousers and a man's shirt. She decided to go out.

"Why not go to the cinema?" she said to herself.

On the embankment of the road from Candé to Ziguinchor the irregular street lamps cast her shadow before her when she passed and behind her as she went on. Alone on this main road she hummed a tune. It was an open air cinema surrounded by a high fence. To enter you passed beneath the screen and faced the raised projection room.

There were two types of seats: benches for the 'natives' and chairs for the Whites. This segregation was partly based on price. Some Africans would have been able to pay for the luxury of a chair but they refused to do so out of solidarity and sat with their brothers.

When she sat on her slightly hard seat, the row was half empty. Yet Isabelle thought she recognised the man from the boat. He was sitting next to another white man who moved next to her with a cheeky, mocking expression: "Madame Faye, will you allow me to sit beside you?"

"I can't prevent you!"

She could sense that the man was looking at her and she kept quiet.

"Are they refusing to let you to talk to Whites? As we are all compatriots I don't think that's very polite. But I won't bite!"

Without replying she took out a cigarette. The man tried to assist her, but Isabelle ignored him. She searched in her pockets and calmly lit her cigarette.

"Yet, my darling, you still don't want to talk," he commented with a half-smile.

From the corner of her eye she observed his straight, cold profile, his chin covered with a 'colonial style' beard which made him look aggressive. His rude stare was hard to tolerate and she finally exploded: "Can't you go back to your place? Your presence disturbs me."

"Go easy, my lovely. Everyone here has paid for their seat."

"Vous m'ennuyez! You're bothering me! That's what you say in French isn't it?"

"I thought you were speaking nigger French."

She slapped him violently. Stunned, they all returned to their seats. She could not understand clearly what the Blacks sitting around her were saying in their language. She could just pick out the word 'Madame'. She knew that this was the nickname they had given her.

Gomis came running, looking worried: "What's going on? Outside they told me that …"

He didn't complete the sentence but, turning towards the white man, he said in a scornful tone: "Listen, Jacques, if her husband hears about this he'll cut you in pieces … you idiot, do you think everyone is a tart?"

The other man did not reply but haughtily stood up and went out.

Hoping Isabelle would forget this event, Gomis said: "I saw you coming in but I was waiting for Agbo and Agnes .... Oh, there they are. Which are your seats?" he asked them both.

"In the second row," said the rather overweight black girl who answered to the name of Agnes.

Gomis introduced everyone to each other. Agbo asked: "What happened to you, Madame Faye?"

"I didn't know this person…"

"It doesn't matter. You slapped him. He deserved it."

Agnes observed: "If your hand is as nimble as your husband's, how's it going to be at your home?"

Agnes was one of those liberated girls who feared nothing. Her companions treated her as a friend but they also feared her sharp tongue. The young ones were still talking as they took their seats.

"You know we travelled here together from Dakar but as we were stuck on deck we hardly ever saw each other," said Agbo.

"Even you?"

Agnes mocked him: "Yes sure, him too, since he didn't pay for a cabin."

Gomis smiled. "Forgive her. She's always like that."

"And what about your husband?"

"Gone fishing with Uncle Amadou."

"What a stick in the mud, he hardly ever goes out with his friends."

Isabelle replied: "And you, will you come and see us on Sunday?"

"Is that an invitation?"

"Yes, Agnes."

"Okay, I'll come."

Agbo was surprised: "But you have to go to Boutoupa."

"No, I've changed my mind."

At this moment the lights went out. The newsreel was followed by a documentary and finally the film itself. It was a cowboy film full of gunshots and perilous situations from which the hero always escaped unhurt. The young star ended up beating the outlaws, winning the heart of the beautiful girl and kissing her in a blaze of glory. Westerns are eternally seductive!

The group chatted as they left the cinema.

"It seems your house is very attractive?"

Agnes was still mocking him. "Doctor, that's an indiscreet question."

"It's terrible, this girl never opens her mouth without causing everyone else to shut theirs."

"Would you like to make a booking for Sunday's visit?" Isabelle asked the doctor.

But he made his apologies. "Thank you but I've a lot to do tomorrow and it's getting late."

"You call that work!" Agnes imitated how the doctor dealt with his patients, simpering: "Where do you feel pain, my pet? Specially for you, here's a packet of aspirin and then afterwards we can …. No, but just listen to him," she said, laughing.

They all made fun of the Dahomeyan.

"Typical kids. When they don't see their friends they look for them and then they never stop teasing each other. Here we are, we've arrived."

They could see nothing but the white zinc of the roof.

"Let's go. Good night, Isabelle. Come on, guys," the girl commanded.

After a few steps they turned back, looking at the house.

"Do come on Sunday, Agbo. You'll have plenty of time."

"Faye is going to be bugged by the others," Agbo

responded. "You've seen how 'they' have already started with his wife …"

"Don't worry …. As far as his wife's concerned, I don't know anything, but for him, nobody can push him around. Anyway he's well established. These are not womanisers who behave like him. All one can say is that this is a real man."

"You fancy him? He's not bad."

"He's not my type. Despite his calm exterior he's too violent. Lots of our compatriots have done what he's done. Married to white girls, they've only just arrived when their wives ditch them … race attracts race."

"That's life."

"Hey guys, this is where we part company," said Agnes. And she disappeared into the night.

The first cock crow woke the women who, beating energetically, made the sound of the pestle resonate in the mortar. Here and there dogs were barking in the distance. Inside their homes the ashes had grown cold. Children who were too young to stay up late or too old to have a lie in were given a slap to wake them up. Morning greetings were restarting the routine of African life.

People were coming from all directions, flocking towards the market. Some had been on their way since the middle of the night to be sure of a good pitch; some arrived by pirogue; some were naked or wearing only a tiny loin cloth. Bit by bit the market was filled with people of all the tribes of the region. Some had their teeth filed to a point, some had closely cropped hair or locks greased with fat. Skin colour varied: albinos with blond eyelashes; 'Portuguese' terra cotta; and darkest black. In the sky above the brightly coloured costumes, the hubbub of voices and the mixture of dialects, the first glimmer of morning was appearing.

The market place was in the centre of the township. One hall was reserved for the butchers and fishmongers. Another was for sellers of precious stones, fabrics from England and from Portugal imported by Hausa, those indefatigable salesmen, or by Bambara. In between these two buildings, on the ground or on raffia mats were decorated calabashes, all kinds of hides, unknown roots, powders to cure any number of illnesses, various fruits, eggs of different types – of chickens and ostriches, and not forgetting crocodiles. It was a Tower of Babel, an African forum. In this anthill where humans and animals mingled, the screams of children and the barking of dogs competed with the cries of the marketeers.

Permission to have a space at the market was granted anew each day. This never failed to annoy the market ladies. Paying money at such an early hour brought bad luck. The art of bargaining was the main skill here. There were no fixed prices.

Normally when Isabelle would arrive at her husband's stall she would find Oumar there. There were two men in between the father and son. Isabelle came up to her father-in-law wishing him, "Bonjour, Papa!" He was selling fish to a Koniadi man dressed only in a loin cloth. Whether the old man did not hear her or he did not want to reply, he continued to negotiate with his customer. Faye's place was empty. One of the men nearby offered Isabelle a stool and with his hand indicated that she should wait there. Doubtless he wanted to explain Faye's unusual lateness but, unable to speak the language, he just smiled as politely as he could and got on with his work. Isabelle waited for a moment, then stood up and moved, passing again near Moussa. She had the impression that the old man was watching her.

"Bonsour, Madame," came a jolly voice from behind her.

"Gosh, Seyna …. Good morning."

The girl gestured to her to wait. She ran towards her father and returned a moment later. She was speaking to Isabelle, who still found her words incomprehensible. Seynabou, still unable to make herself understood, pulled Isabelle by the wrist. They inspected a part of the market where the crush was even greater and stopped there. A gourd wrought in molten iron attracted Isabelle's attention. She decided to purchase it. At once the black woman started bargaining.

"How much are you selling this gourd for?"

"Oh, my dear, this masterpiece, this charming little calabash. I'll give it to you for a hundred francs."

"Gosh, that's too expensive, much too expensive." Saying this Seynabou took the gourd from her sister-in-law's hands and handed it back.

"Listen, girl, it's not for you, it's for your employer. So if we split the difference what'll be left for us? Ask her for one hundred and fifty and the fifty will be for you."

"She's not my employer. She's my spouse..." (In Senegal a brother's wife is considered to be the spouse of all the brothers and sisters.)

"Sorry then. What is your offer?"

"Fifty francs and here's the cash," said Seynabou.

"No, child, forget it. That means you don't want to buy it. This morning I refused an offer of seventy-five francs." She spoke angrily, pointing down at the ground.

They moved away. The market woman spat as they went but she called them back: "Well then, take it and give me eighty francs."

"Fifty!"

The woman pondered, counted on her fingers, pulled a face and finally gave in: "Give me sixty-five francs. I could be your mother. That's why I've agreed to sell at a loss. Perhaps you have luck on your side for I've sold nothing since I got here …. Is it true that she's the wife of your brother?" she asked with astonishment.

"If I say so!"

"I believe you. But then, doesn't she understand anything we're saying?"

"Nothing."

Looking at Isabelle she said: "The poor woman. She seems nice. You can tell her that I have prettier ones and that if she would like any I can sell them to her …. And the poor thing. The truth is that we are all parents!"

They paid. Seynabou pointed to the market woman: "Woman. Parler beaucoup, very cunning."

When they got back the fishermen were still not there, which made Isabelle very worried. She hesitated to speak to her father-in-law. She was really afraid of him. Since her arrival at Fayene the only words they had exchanged were on that first day. Isabelle did not know why this man showed such hostility towards her. The hour passed and her worries about Faye increased. She wondered what to do? No longer able to stay silent any longer, she turned to the old man.

"Oumar?"

He bent his head with a gesture indicating that he knew nothing. Yet it was inconceivable that men who went fishing at the normal time and with absolutely nothing to worry about should not return. Crocodiles? This would not be the first time, but best not to think about that …. Those watching on the quays scanned the narrow entrance to the harbour for any sign. People had heard that some fishermen had not returned and it was the silence rather than spoken comments that expressed everyone's solidarity. Still nothing on the horizon. The market seemed to be holding its breath. The only sound was the wind that was issuing a muted groan.

Others had come to swell the ranks of the first arrivals, some seated on the wooden slats with their feet dangling into the water. The usual optimism that filled this place at this time of day was accompanied by the anxiety of those more superstitious. Isabelle, in the middle of the crowd, lit a cigarette to give herself composure, but anxiety gnawed at her throat. She went to sit alone on a parapet at the far end of the port, fixing all her attention on the luminous horizon.

Ten loud peals came from the nearby church. Seeing that time was passing, an emergency team was put together. Moussa and several others organised some pirogues. At this moment the crowd noticed a black spot in the middle of the estuary. Soon, a man could be seen disembarking, but when they recognised it was Amadou they worried again, seeing him with his forearm entwined in mangrove branches and lying next to this sea monster which was a great deal taller than him.

One careless onlooker fell into the water, which provoked general hilarity. Moussa helped his brother climb up and he gave orders to his son.

"What happened to you?" asked Isabelle, elbowing her way to get near to her husband.

"A shark ….Do you have a pipe?"

In a few words he told her about their adventure, laughing out loud and displaying the creature as a trophy in the public square. The story of what had happened spread rapidly.

Oumar went through the crowd to his sales pitch. Isabelle leant on him, trying to hold his hand. As she was sitting down, suddenly a voice made her tremble. "Good day, Madame." Lifting her head she first saw some sandals, bare, hairy legs, khaki shorts, a 'colonial' shirt and a white helmet. Faye recognised Raoul, his adversary on the boat. He clenched his teeth, the veins on his forehead swelled and he readied his fist, but he controlled himself.

"I've a message for you from Jacques. Maybe the name means nothing to you? He's the white man you were with yesterday at the cinema. He's interested in you and when someone gets under his skin he goes all the way.... Otherwise, you know, he's not a bad man."

He said all this in a syrupy tone. Isabelle's lips trembled. Oumar put his hand on his wife's shoulder, a gesture that the manager of Cosono noticed, and he followed, speaking directly to Faye: "Young man, I think we know each other. You are a rare person in this town, but I haven't come for you today .... I've got my eye on you all the same but there's nothing to fear."

All his hatred had flared up in his eyes but, like a chameleon, this expression immediately disappeared.

Faye went up to him.

"Listen to what I am saying ... people of your type are harmful for black people, but even more so for their own race. Next time I'll make you swallow your words. And I promise you you'll end up keeping your gob shut. As far as she's concerned, I'm not saying anything. She's there, isn't she? When someone descends so low it disgusts me. If you want to have a good share of the catch, come back tomorrow."

"Talking of sales, how much do you want for the catch?"

"For you? I'd rather let it rot."

The white man shrugged his shoulders contemptuously.

"A shame. You would have got a good price." And off he went.

As if nothing had happened, Faye went to a young black woman who was selling straw hats. He chose one and brought it to his wife: "Have this. Don't imagine you are already acclimatised to the sun."

"About this man, do you believe what he said?"

"No,"

"Why are they so beastly?"

"They have to humiliate so that they drive me to the point where I become their victim a second time. Because … firstly I don't have the right to live, to have feelings, to love, to carve myself a place in the sun. They don't want me to cross the line and if I resist them they will be sure to get rid of me …. And, they cannot tolerate a black man having sex with a white woman. That flouts their laws."

He stopped and was calm again. Isabelle said nothing.

After the market closed they went to pay a visit to Fayene. Spasmodic groans could be heard from the dark room; the tears of the women created a gloomy atmosphere that evening. Moussa called his son into his room. He was on a mat reciting the Koran. The old man took his time to speak: "Your wife came to the market without greeting me. Don't you think this was bad?"

"She told me the contrary."

"Ah, so I'm a liar?"

Oumar did not know how to reply. In Africa you do not contradict your father. Yet he was quite certain that Isabelle had not lied to him.

"You know that she doesn't tell the truth. Whites are always like that. Believe me, my son, I've known them longer than you have. Their words have as much value as chicken shit …"

This conversation was becoming unbearable for Faye. He was angry with his father and he wanted him to hurry up and stop talking. But what tortured him the most was that Moussa could say anything that crossed his mind, while he had to be content with acquiescing. With a sense of relief

Faye left his father and joined Isabelle back at the table with his mother.

Rokhaya asked: "What did your father say?"

"He talked about God," replied Oumar pensively, scratching the nape of his neck.

"You know he's right. You were born a believer and brought up with the commandments of the Koran. You can read the white man's book equally well but you have never bowed down in prayer …. If you die tomorrow what will you do, my son? You won't be young for ever."

"Mother, who tells you that I don't pray?"

"You do, yes, but only when someone dies …. I don't want you to pray for me."

"Oh … I don't want to pray for you just yet!" and he put his arms round Rokhaya's shoulders.

"Son of a dog," she murmured, "what did I do to the Good God that he gave me a dog."

"Am I not a good son?"

She evaded the question. "What are you going to do now? Are you going to work in an office?"

"No. I'm going to start farming?"

She was stupefied: "What? There have never been farmers in my family, nor in your father's, nor in his father's."

"From now on you won't be able to say that anymore."

"God. God, my God!" Rokhaya lamented, rubbing her face with her hands. "And your uncle? Is he going to be left alone? He's not in very good health."

"Mother, it's nothing serious. I've done what's needed …. What has Massiré said?"

"First of all I beg you to call him Papa Massiré."

In the face of this hostility which did not abate, Oumar said to Isabelle that they would leave.

Rokhaya, seeing them go, cried: "Go, then go away, son

of a dog."

Laughing, they disappeared – towards the palm trees.

"What did my mother say to you?" Faye asked his wife, "Did you understand what she said?"

"Not much ... God, the Koran ..."

"Yes," he said, "my father wanted you to become a Muslim."

There was a silence.

"And you, what do you think?"

"To tell the truth, that doesn't thrill me; and to start with you don't know anything about it ..."

"I can learn," she said.

"You know, I'd be allowed to have four wives."

"Oh, really? That rules it out then. But tell me first, did you use to pray?"

"It was when I was at the battlefront that I understood it was bullshit. There are people who have never missed a single prayer – and yet they've been left out in the cold."

"Your parents," said Isabelle, "will think it's my fault."

"You're not going to live with them ... and, anyway, I believed this matter to be solved between you and me."

"That's true."

"So, just protect us from evil, and may God help us to stop worrying about it."

Both became silent again. Oumar was pensive.

After a pause Oumar resumed: "You and I have received a different education, as different as the colour of our skins. A single misunderstanding would be enough to smash our relationship. Never forget that we are living in two worlds, between the day and the night. No black and no white person can imagine that we are really capable of understanding each other. You have seen how I have been received, even in my own home, even among my family. And when I met your mother for the first time after we had known each other for five months do you remember how my pride was wounded? The earth was not deep enough to bury me at that moment. Happily your father was more understanding."

"For my part, I can't say anything different!"

"Exactly," said Faye. "But now we have our own home. Let's forget the others."

Before they realised where they were they had arrived at La Palmeraie.

PART TWO

Chapter 1

Oumar had worked out that it was only a matter of days before the start of the rainy season. Just a few warm breaths of air could be felt in the atmosphere. The clouds were not moving. The young man was still going on his long walks through the open bush. Always barefoot, he trampled the vegetation as he walked. He had made a note of all the trees around La Palmeraie. The nomads who lived nearby were wondering if this son of a fisherman had not gone mad. They were astonished at his wanderings. It was said that he had been heard talking to himself on more than one occasion. But Oumar was totally intoxicated by the natural world and could never have enough of it. His eyes had first seen daylight in this country; he knew that he was moulded out of this, his very own soil. His skin was impregnated with its aroma. Since childhood he had been rubbed in it from head to toe. Ah, how he loved the earth, this earth, his own earth, and how he cherished it! He was jealous of it. He compared it to a woman who both loved and was loved. The trees were her hair, the soil was her flesh, the rocks were her bones, the streams were her blood and their sources her eyes. Her mouth was a ripe fruit, the hills her breasts. He imagined invisible hands and arms defending themselves, surrendering and then clasping in a tight embrace. The forest was her mysterious headdress, her support, her strength as well as her weakness; and for her voice she had the wind, the thunder and the soft murmurings of the night.

The forest was a good mother and a brave woman, but at times she rebels because she enjoys the regular, brutal, beating of the *conco* on the ground.

This is how Oumar came to terms with the first steps of the life of a farmer. Days and weeks meant little to him at this time: his existence was ruled only by the seasons. And Oumar would have gone further into the bush had he not just remembered that in fact Isabelle had invited some friends.

Seeing him she cried: "Ah, there you are, wanderer. You leave all the work for me to do … go on, lazybones …. Look. I've written to my parents," she added as he entered the house.

She disappeared into the kitchen after handing him the letter.

Ziguinchor, the…

My dear parents,

I have not broken the promise I made before my departure. In fact, even if I have not written to you very often I have at least sent heaps of telegrams. So don't worry, my health is very good and so is that of the Big Man.

When we arrived we only stayed one night in his father's house and then we camped for two months. The Big Man has worked very hard and I have helped him as best I could. With the sweat of our brows we have built our own home. It's a sort of bungalow built of poto-poto, the local name for a kind of cob – mud and straw. We had lots of discussions about the construction and finally we divided the job: I worked on the ground floor including the kitchen and he, my lord and master, on the first floor and the roofing.

So here I am, a Casamancienne and I'm not complaining. Our house is on the shore of a backwater. From every window we can see trees and at full moon we enjoy the gleaming reflection of the great river.

As I have had little leisure before our guests arrive I'm going to tell you about my in-laws. Oumar's father has three wives of which the first is my mother-in-law. She is a strange lady with a reputation of being something of a clairvoyant. We speak rarely with each other – and never with his father who is a kind of preacher at the mosque.

Since I arrived I have been seen as a kind of intruder and this has not changed. I hope this does not continue for too long, and for the moment I am not sharing my apprehensions with Oumar. What does not make things easy is that up to now I have only been able to learn a few sentences in the local dialects which are innumerable. Otherwise the Big Man's parents disapprove of their son's attitude: firstly because he married a white woman and then because he does not accept their conception of the clan. The family plays an enormous role here. Everything is in common and nothing is really individual. When you give something it is understood that if tomorrow someone needs to take it, they can do so.

Also I think there is a third reason that I am not very welcome: it's that our two countries are not fully sovereign. I'm copying a sentence from a book by a Chinese writer whose name I forget which will enable you to understand what I mean: 'In countries placed under foreign domination individuals lose their creative power bit by bit, and from one generation to another their energy diminishes.' I am not sure if one day I will be understood, but for the moment I'm learning to know my husband's people, I share his anxieties – but also his optimism.

Dear parents, you know that there is a great difference between the Blacks we learn about in the classroom or see performing in shows and those living in their own home. We are quite often visited by a group of friends, almost all young, and that's how I'm noticing the changes which are taking place at the present time. The stereotype of the idle, nonchalant African with no care for tomorrow is gradually disappearing along with the older generation. Young people give the impression of having a clearer idea of where they want to go. I don't know if I'm explaining this well but this is what I'm starting to feel.

Otherwise everything is going well here. I would love it if you could come and spend one or two months with us. In the meantime write to us a bit more often. Is life still as expensive as ever in Paris? From that point of view this place is a paradise.

What's the news of Louise? Does she go out dancing a lot? Oumar has a half-sister of the same age whose name is Seynabou.

There's a real plague of mosquitoes here. Despite our mosquito nets we are overrun by them. Do something for us. Send some products to protect us from these foul creatures.

Lots of love from us both,
Mme Oumar Faye,
Route de Candé - La Palmeraie

As he was reading, Isabelle came to sit beside him on the divan. Oumar put the letter in the envelope, sealed it and stretched out beside her.

"You've never told me about your fears," he said.

"I didn't want to hurt you."

"Doesn't that show a lack of confidence?"

"Don't say that!" Isabelle hit back, "Forgive me if I did something wrong but don't begin to question my feelings."

Faye did not like emotional language. Cheerfully he said, "Your guests are about to arrive. I must get myself ready."

Sliding down the smooth slope of the sky the thinning clouds were turning a bluish hue, like the colour of indigo in soapy water. Far off above the trees a tall band of flaming sky threw sulphurous arrows into the bright, blood-red horizon.

That Sunday nearly all the young friends came to La Palmeraie. Most of them were dressed smartly except for M'Boup and Seck Dieng. Agnes, wearing a brightly coloured dress, was accompanied by two very attractive girls. Everyone sat down as best they could, some on chairs, others on the steps of the sitting room. Drinks were passed round. Isabelle, dressed in a tartan skirt and a short-sleeved blouse, was serving rice cakes. Diagne was on the bottom step, talking loudly of his experiences: "You see, my dear friends, there is nothing better and more pleasant than to spend a Sunday afternoon in the company of beautiful girls. I swear it's true, you judge a woman by her food. Today reminds me of Saint-Louis of Senegal, the birthplace of African civilisation. The art of playing host to men is uniquely the concern of women. Don't be surprised if Loti stays longer than she needs to. That's true isn't it, my beauty?" he asked the girl sitting on the settee where he was pontificating.

"I don't know anything about it," she replied in a timid voice.

Agnes intervened: "Say nothing more, Rosaline. He's starting his tactical advances."

"Thank you, my sister, for making my job easier!"

"Tell me, Monsieur Faye…" But the doctor had gone no further when Oumar cut him short.

"Doctor, among ourselves we don't use the word 'Monsieur'…"

Agbo spoke calmly, putting one leg over the other: "I see, are you one of those who say that politeness is based on hypocrisy?"

"That may be true," said Faye.

Isabelle touched her husband's elbow, thinking he had offended Agbo: "Excuse my husband, doctor. You must have misunderstood each other?"

"I agree with him," replied Agbo, taking a sip from his glass.

At this moment a white man burst into the room. Agbo stood up and introduced him: "Joseph, a specialist in tropical diseases." The conversation froze. The new arrival feared he was the cause of this.

Faye spoke: "Dr Joseph, where did you do your studies?"

"In Paris at the Saint-Louis Hospital, then a year at the Pharo in Marseille. Do you know Marseille?"

"No."

One of the group cut in angrily: "It appears to be a city of hoodlums and bandits. Many of our compatriots have had a bad time there."

The teacher, who had not yet spoken, responded: "Young man, don't forget the saying, 'The wind that blows the leaves into the ditch doesn't blow them away.'"

Pensively, Agnes replied: "Me, I have an uncle who has lived there for years; he writes often to my mother. He's married and is the father of three kids …. Ah!" she sighed with hope in her voice, "I'd love to be able to visit France …"

The teacher recited:

Why, happy child
Why leave our sweet country
For overcrowded cities,
To harvest more suffering,
To entrust yourself to bullies,
To bid fond farewell to our dear baobabs?
You, half clothed here,
There, shivering in the snow,
As you will miss our drums,
Our open-hearted laughter,
And if your body is held in pitiless constraint
You would have to beg for your dinner
By selling the sweetness of your flesh,
In the foul weather with your eye dreaming
Of the bulky shadows of absent trees.

The ovation was sincere. Touched, the schoolmaster stood up and took a bow which was out of keeping with his rough and grumpy manner. He dreamed of going to the theatre, even if it was only once, to see "Romeo and Juliet". Seck knew that the verse he had recited was not by Shakespeare.

"I could talk more about it, and more beautifully," said the descendant of the Moors.

After a silence, Gomis said: "We're listening."

"Agnes, you keep quiet or go for a walk."

"He's going to talk nonsense. It's the only thing he knows how to do!"

He responded gravely: "Thank you." He began: "True or not, it is very hard to confirm it to you. It happened in

Senegal, or perhaps in Niger or in Soudan (Mali) or in Ivory Coast, why not?"

"Go on, speak for God's sake! No monkeying about!" said M'Boup.

"You see, my secretary is panicking, so … 'In the early days of colonisation a couple of Whites were close friends with a native. The months and years passed and their relationship grew stronger. One day, alas, as happens to us all…"

Diagne paused and felt in his pockets.

"Who's giving me one? A yellow one of course."

"There you are, my brother," said Faye.

"Thank you, brother-in-law, I will marry your sister."

"For the price of a cigarette? Seyna is cheap," grumbled Agnes.

"Just a minute! … I'm continuing. Where was I? Oh yes. Then, as I said, things happen. The white settler dies and his wife was very cut up about it, as was the black man. A few days later the good lady gave some money to our hero to buy a wreath to put on the grave of 'Monsieur'. The next day she nearly fell over with shock when she saw the man coming with the wreath of flowers around his neck.

'Didn't you understand that they were to be put on his grave?' she said.

He opened his eyes wide and made gestures that the widow did not understand.

Then he said, 'There are flowers on Monsieur,' and he pointed his finger at his stomach.'"

The African doctor was shocked: "Do you always have such ideas?"

"Is my story in bad taste?"

"No," replied Agnes. "As I said at the beginning. He

doesn't know anything good!"

"So, let's say it's the thought that counts."

Every Sunday they made a date at La Palmeraie, some-times even on a weekday evening. These days their presence was missed at the main square. At the Fayes' they found the friendly 'Madame' serving *N'iangkalang* or *Dempéting*.

Heat, pungent and suffocating, seemed to cling to every-body and gave them the sensation of being bogged down in a sweat that accumulated under the armpits and the nape of the neck and then trickled over the whole body.

A black cloud darkened the east and spread above the city. It moved until it covered the whole of the sky, merging with the red disc of the sun. The huts returned to their original shade of earthen grey and were soon obscured in the half-light. Then without warning a wind blew from the bush, rustled the leaves on the trees, made the palm fronds sway gently and refreshed faces that were clammy with perspiration.

In the sky, coming from afar and moving in a rapid zigzag, lightning flashed and was quickly lost in the depths of the void. Homes were shaken by the shock of thunder. It made the earth tremble. The hurricane had arrived as it had in years past. The wide ocean of the air was getting ready to produce a tempest. Majestic and solemn, gusts of air burst forth, thrusting and carrying away everything in their path. The more flexible trees bowed down to make the ceremony appear more serious. The pattering on the corrugated zinc of the roofs was the sign that the rain had started.

From all directions people rushed home, animals disap-peared into holes beneath the hedges. The blustering wind died down. No sound but the rapid beat of rain hitting the ground, the murmur of the treetops and the deep groans of the coconut and toddy palms as it struck in its frenzy;

the loud orchestration of the storm was only penetrated by the happy screams of kids, frolicking under the torrents of water. The tornado was sweeping away everything. Things were whirling about in crazy disorder. Nothing was visible more than a short distance away. It was impossible to walk without bending double.

In their bedroom Oumar and his wife had closed everything. He was obsessed with his thoughts and seemed not to be worried by the infernal racket that was going on outside, but 'Madame's' gaze indicated wonder and a certain amount of apprehension as she watched the outside world between the two shutters at the window.

"This rain. There's going to be more of it."

"I'm frightened," she said.

He turned back to put her mind at rest: "Come here, for it's going on all day and all night."

She sighed: "And it's only three o'clock."

"I've an idea. Why not take a shower?"

"In the rain?"

"No, under the roof," he said mockingly.

"I'm game!"

With their accustomed nudity they submitted to the rain, splashing themselves like little brats. Their frolics went on for a time. Then abruptly "something" crossed their narrow line of vision, the thunderclap shook the house, the storm lashed the windows. It tried to pull the house to pieces, reverberating as though tons and tons of rock were hurtling down a mountainside. Each thunderclap was such that it was incomprehensible that such a diaphanous substance as water could have such power. The wind rose up to great heights only to beat down again on the ground with all its vigour. Oumar, at the doorway, was admiring nature unleashed. Isabelle, dripping wet, came to join him. While they were drying themselves a gust of wind burst into the house and shook the walls. Faye hastily pushed his wife indoors and slammed the door shut. Now the wind rattled the door.

"We'll be lucky if the house doesn't collapse!"

Fitfully the speed of the wind's attack increased. The roof suffered stronger attacks, repeated at regular intervals. Shamelessly the gusts, as fluid as ether and strong as steel, were searching for fissures and cracks which they could continue to work to widen into wide breaches in the walls. Here and there the wind penetrated beneath the zinc sheets and lifted them like wisps of straw, tossing them noisily as though they were unwanted sheets of paper into the trees and onto the pathway.

Then came the night, a black night fraught with agitated silhouettes and frightened cries while the wind unrelentingly attacked high and low in the darkness. After each flash of lightning the growls of thunder grew ever louder. This night when all the elements were in revolt left an incredible impression.

"I've never seen such weather."

"That was nothing. It wasn't a really big storm."

"Oh you, you always exaggerate!"

They were hidden under the mosquito net that covered the bed. The only light in the room was the feeble glow of a paraffin lamp, turned down low. Some cigarette smoke escaped through the gauze.

"Give me the fag."

"Do you remember when you told me that the rain in France was nothing compared to the rain in Africa?"

"Pass me that fag," he repeated.

"Damn it, wait a bit or take one yourself."

"There are none left."

"I've got some in my bag, go and look."

"Oh, that's where you hide them, is it?"

"There's the fag, there it is, you brute, you savage, you cannibal!"

The ending of the night was unbelievable. The storm was still in control, blowing into people's homes through broken doors, showing off its power by making the roofing fly into the air like feathers. It carried off everything, even huts, leaving nothing in its wake apart from poor, unhappy homeless folk for whom the hours that followed were hard and very long.

Breaking through the storm, a weak patch of light signalled the approach of dawn. An hour before daybreak there was a lull. This was sudden and with no warning sign, just as it had been when the storm started . The tumult had run its full course and all at once it was silenced. As though it was gasping, the wind breathed its last, giving way to a gloomy emptiness. The water receded from where it had flooded. It surged back, gushing headlong towards the river, through people's homes, beneath the roots of great trees or over tree trunks that blocked its turbulent flow, carrying with it a load of flotsam, shrouded in a curtain of mist.

The flow moved at an incredible speed; all kinds of debris was floating on its surface. The ditches bordering the embankments were a scene of wild disorder of foaming and swirling torrents. The river, normally clear and green, was dark yellow.

The sun followed the storm. Already moths and flying ants were flying here and there, to the great delight of the children who were enjoying getting bogged down in the soft clay. The women were hanging clothes soaked by the storm on what was left of the fencing.

Very early in the morning Oumar inspected the house.

"I thought the hurricane had carried you away and I

imagined myself already a widow," said Isabelle.

"Oh hell, a good hiding in the morning wouldn't hurt you!"

She prepared breakfast. As he was eating Faye said: "You must learn to remain here at home. Another thing, don't ever go out without doing your hair. And then don't forget to write to your father and to tend the young plants."

"Yes boss," she replied with her elbows on the table. "And you, don't forget to get home by twelve and bring some cigarettes."

"Really, you beat all the records! You have to have my shirts, my pants, my cigarettes, and what else?"

"Me, I'm not selfish! You can wear my skirts if you like!"

He gave a tug to her long hair saying, "See you later."

Everywhere ahead of him it was not only pools of water and scattered heaps of refuse that he could see. Fayene was partly destroyed. Everyone was up and about, with the exception of Uncle Amadou who was overcome by what had happened and was groaning and begging for God's mercy. Oumar helped to fix the doors and windows and to mend the roof.

"My son, how is it at your place?" her mother asked, ejecting a large mouthful of spit onto the wet ground.

"Good, I've not had any damage."

"And 'Madame'?"

"She's well too."

"I've not seen such a rainstorm for a long time. I advise you not to go swimming any more. I've seen some evil spirits."

"What do you want me to do about it if your spirits want to move around?"

"You are not a white man."

"Agreed." He looked at her and then a moment later:

"Mother, I need a lot of money."

"To do what?"

"For my work as a farmer."

"Why do you want to become a farmer? Not only do you not live here with us but you want to work. It's strange."

"I want to do it for you, for everybody."

"If we waited for you to provide food we would die of hunger. You know nothing about the soil."

"It's true. I know nothing about the soil. I have to learn."

"Your father and your father's father were all fishermen, but you, the toubaab, you want the soil. I just don't understand."

"That's true!"

"Are you telling your mother she's lying! You, you are civilised. You don't want to dirty your hands eating with us!"

"Then thank you, mother, I don't want your money anymore."

"There you are, you call me a liar and then you get angry. Definitely, nothing I say pleases you. Sometimes I wonder if you don't just want to become white."

"See you tomorrow, mother. I'll see my father at the market. At least he doesn't want to say anything."

He knew his mother well. He knew that to obtain anything from her he had to push her to the limit and leave her with the angry words still on her lips.

Sitting on the mortar, she called him: "Oumar, come back. It would have been better to crush you at birth. If I do that now the toubaabs like you would put me in prison. How much do you want?"

"Everything you've got."

"Go on, go away, you dog!"

"Money has no roots but it grows in the heart."

He went out but she ran after him and caught him. She walked beside him, though he pretended not to see her.

"Perhaps I'm just wittering on," she said, "it's just that there's not a big difference between the past and the present. Don't get cross if I talk nonsense. You see, for me you are still my little boy. And when you were in Tugal and I was waiting for you, I felt a weight next to my heart as though you were still in my womb. Now you have come back I am worried about you and your wife. People talk a lot ..."

In silence he listened to his mother's words and to the rustling of her costume. She went on: "Perhaps I am moaning for no reason. I get so worried that my mind is a blank. When I see you, like I do now, I want to follow you, and when you're out of sight my heart stops. I've stopped thinking anymore and there's nothing more I can do. I say to myself: 'If he comes back and says that he is returning to the land of the toubaabs for ever ...' Ah, that would kill me! God knows that I don't hate your Madame, but I beg you that if one day she wanted to go then let her go alone. Don't abandon your old mother. I have not much time left in this world. She seems kind, your Madame, though we don't speak the same language. Does she understand me? Oh, don't go back there, don't abandon your aged mother ..."

"I will not go, mother, I promise you that ..."

"I pray to the angels and to the great prophet that this idea never takes root in your head. My little one, it's just that you are my only, my unique possession in this world."

"So have no fear for me. I will never cause you to feel shame. Just don't pay attention to what people tell you."

"I'm pleased to hear you say that," she said, holding his hand as she did when he took his first steps. "Come, let's go to Papa Gomis."

Old Gomis was the man they trusted. As they entered his

shop he came to meet them. He was always ready to listen to them. Henceforth, this is where Oumar had to come if he needed help.

Faye parted from his mother, promising to do nothing wrong. He went to walk through the market, greeting people here and there, then rather aimlessly he wandered along the quay. Three vessels had cast anchor. Women were loading one of the three boats which were at the far end of the pier. Faye watched them working. This scene was nothing new to him. He had seen it as a child. Nonetheless he felt a twinge of sorrow. It was wrong, it was odious that women drudged in this way! The fact that nobody reacted against this state of affairs made him feel very uneasy. He knew he was partly to blame for the sluggish progress in the country; and what's more he was doing nothing about it.

The women did not seem to be unhappy. Following orders, they moved in single file with the sacks of groundnuts straining their neck muscles. Their torsos were half naked and their skin dull, marked by a stream of perspiration to which was added a coating of red dust around the waist. There were girls with perfect bodies and old women with flattened breasts under their wrappers. They had to walk past a man who was seated and gave them a token for each sack.

"Why don't you employ men?" Oumar asked him.

The man raised his head to see who was speaking to him. Without speaking he continued handing out the tokens.

"Why?"

"That's my problem!" He spoke in French in a tone that was not at all friendly. "… Anyway, who are you?"

Oumar was surprised … "Who am I? I'm a man like you. You're right. This is not my problem."

"So…?"

91

"So, I am saying that this work would be better done by men rather than women. Look at this
girl. Isn't it shameful? And this old woman with her head shaved. She's old enough to be your mother although she's black. Do you think it's like this in Syria?"

"Speak politely if you don't want to regret it. First of all I am not a Syrian."

"You are as much a Syrian as I am a black man — from your head to your toes. Between you and me, if I talk like this it's to help your business. It's not long since you arrived from your village. No Syrians are doing your kind of work. I know all of them."

The other man did not reply. He merely watched Faye, stung by his words which were both calm
and brutal. Oumar only had eyes for one girl who was leading the group. She was singing, but she sounded oppressed. Her life had taught her to sing as a way of shutting out reality. Singing together, these women sang to stifle their sobs – so they could forget their exhaustion. They sang as they do at circumcisions, and it was not a song of joy but of sadness; it began as it ended. It incarnated wretchedness … and their wretchedness was never ending.

Unable to keep staring at her for ever, Oumar called the girl. They spoke together for some time.
The supervisor got angry.

"Listen my friend. She's not working for you any longer. Here, take back the tokens," he added forcefully.

"She's leaving? Okay she won't be paid if the boat isn't fully loaded."

"I'll wait till this evening."
The women crowded around them and watched wide eyed. At this point a man came to find out what had happened and why work had stopped.

"Why don't these black women want to work?"

"You see, boss, it's this guy who has taken away the best worker among them."

The captain of the ship spoke first to Faye: "Come here, you. Bosco, bring me the chicotte. He'll see who's in charge here." Faye was in no doubt that he was about to be beaten. Armed with his whip, the commander advanced towards him.

"Why have you stopped my work?"

"Are you carrying a whip because you want to speak to me?"

"So, you speak French? See here, there's a black who speaks like us. Have a look at this nigger."
And he whipped him on the face. Faye raised both hands to his face where the whip had bitten into his skin. He received another blow to his back and then he was kicked. The other dock workers were having a good laugh. The commander turned towards the dockers who were keen to continue the attack.

"Now, you others, if all the work is not finished today nobody will be paid. As for you, monkey escaped from the zoo, make sure I never see you here again …"

But he did not have time to finish speaking. Two hands grabbed his neck. He turned pale. Faye sent him rolling on the ground. As soon as he stood up, a punch struck him on the back of the neck. Blood was spurting. The crowd retreated onto the wharf, frightened at the sight of the white man covered in blood. Men from his crew arrived to give aid to their boss and Faye withdrew. There was a shed on the wharf and he pushed against it. The wooden rail that was attached to it yielded. He grabbed hold of it and hit the first of the attackers on the arm.

"Kill this nigger," shouted the blood-soaked commander. But he did not dare come near. The way in which Faye wielded this bludgeon proved that he knew how to make use of it. Another stronger sailor tried his luck. He charged forward. Faye dodged cleverly while not exposing his back to the others. He struck a blow on the left shoulder of his adversary who lost his balance. He renewed the attack, this time on his right shoulder. The man collapsed, spread out full length. Oumar, victorious, who was wearing boots on account of the previous day's rain, put his foot on the head of the recumbent man. Cries and "hurrahs" sounded from the crowd which had assembled on the waterfront.

Someone had provided the commander with a revolver. "Drop your bludgeon or else I'll land on you ... Drop it!", he ordered

Seeing the gun, the onlookers were silent. In the water beneath the shed, carp could be heard snapping up the flotsam that had been brought there by the current. A deathly silence descended on the quay. Faye's eyes were bloodshot and became a terrifying red, and the veins of his forehead and temples were swollen. All of this lasted just one second. The shot was fired and the bullet skimmed across his thigh. Now it was no longer a scuffle but a massacre: the gun and its owner were in the water and the men of the crew fled towards the boat, while the local people shouted the rudest insults they knew in their language. Oumar followed them, lifting his bludgeon.

He could hear nothing more, he could think nothing more, he did not know why he had hit out like this. He was sweating and the blood from his wound was mixing with the sweat. The crew returned armed with batons and the combat resumed. With his powerful arms the black man brandished his bludgeon overhead, swinging it round. As he was starting to feel that his strength was diminishing, he heard that the police commissioner, who had been told in the market what was happening, was arriving with his militia.

"Arrest them all and follow me. Get on with it, to the police station!"

But the ship's captain, who was still soaking wet and bleeding, refused.

"This ape needs to go to prison. He came looking for trouble. I wonder why we educate these savages!"

"Put me in prison, you filthy pig," Faye shouted in his face.

"That's enough," said the voice of law and order.

The young Gomis arrived, out of breath. "What is this?" he asked, "What has happened?"

"Nothing. It's all over," replied Faye.

"You're bleeding, man, and you say it's nothing."

"You keep out of this," said the commissioner.

"I'm not asking for anything," Gomis replied.

"I'm leaving to go to Kaolack this evening," said the captain. "Put him in prison till I return, give him two months."

Gomis exclaimed again "You say so? The time when Blacks were thrown in prison without trial is over."

"Gomis, that's enough. And consider what you are saying," shouted the commissioner, who was starting to lose his patience.

"It's all right, Gomis," said Faye. And turning to speak to the guardian of law and order he said: "It seems that these gentlemen have not made up their minds. I'm going off to nurse my wounds and they can do what they want."

The members of the crew, seeing that the Blacks were not cowed by the simple presence of the police commissioner, returned to their ship.

"Faye, you are becoming a danger to public safety. Next time you can be sure that I will put you in prison."

"Public safety … that's a joke here," replied Oumar.
Gomis and Faye forced a way through the crowd and, as recognition of what he had done, people raised their hands towards Oumar. The girl was following behind them.

"You could say it was because of this girl that I almost stayed there," said Faye. And to her he added: "Come along with us."

Gomis' old jalopy dropped them back at La Palmeraie, but on the way Oumar had fainted. The African doctor had been summoned and he came, accompanied by Joseph Agbo. The news spread rapidly through all parts of the town.

Rokhaya arrived as fast as her old legs could carry her. She was not very happy to see her "little one" being treated by these "doctors" and Gomis had to calm things down by explaining to her that there was nothing else he could do. Isabelle, not knowing what to say, had him carried up to the bedroom. Faye slept. The traces of blood were still fresh on his skin.

"It's nothing serious. He needs rest. He has lost blood but we have administered a fair amount," said Agbo. "Don't allow him to drink water too often, better make him take chicken soup… au revoir, Madame."

"Thank you doctor, Doctor Joseph, thanks again."
Beside the bed his mother was leaning over her son. She took his arm from under the blanket wanting to see the bandage.

"No, mother," said Isabelle, pulling back her arm.

"Malatte beaucoup?"

"No, just tired, finish in three days."

All the time Oumar had to stay in bed there was perfect silence in the house.

That afternoon Oumar and Isabelle were on their veranda. He was rocking slowly on his rocking chair, all the while caressing Isabelle's head which was resting on his shoulder, and with his hands feeling the movement of the two braids that divided her long, soft hair.

A voice surprised them and disturbed their intimacy.

"I see there's hardly any more need for my services."

"Good afternoon, doctor."

"Afternoon all."

Agbo gave a leaf of tobacco to the old lady and then turned towards Faye. "May I look at your wound? Good. It's forming a scar. You can go to work in two days' time. Can I trust you?"

"I don't know."

"This is the first time I've treated a patient outside the hospital."

"I wouldn't wish you to have any other cases, at least not here."

"When I was at school I always dreamed of having my own surgery."

"Don't lose hope, Agbo."

"If everyone was like Mama Rokhaya then it's good-bye to the medical profession!"

"People of Casamance, I salute you!"

These were Diagne's merry words as he arrived unexpectedly along with M'boup, Dieng and Thiam.

"Hey, look at the crazy man! Yesterday he went to a film about ancient Rome and all week he'll be a Roman; but after a western he'll be a cowboy, then he'll play the tough guy …"

The young arrivals laughed as they helped to bring out the tables and chairs. The black girl whom Faye had brought to La Palmeraie served drinks. Her name was Itylima and

'Madame' had given her a skirt and a mauve blouse to wear.

"My brother, the next time you want to have a fight you must let me know. Together …."

"No, Diagne, it's past. Don't let's talk any more about it. It was an accident."

"Anyway you have now become the defender of the weak and the oppressed. Only yesterday a girl asked me for news about you."

"How do you think Africa will ever wake up from its inertia with people around like Diagne?" said Agbo. "Instead of trying to complete their education they spend the evenings looking for new victims to sleep with!"

Diagne in 'staff officer' mode with his elbows on the table spoke pensively this time: "What's the point of educating ourselves? They treat us as undesirables. How many unemployed graduates are there in Dakar, Saint-Louis and Rufisque? I can read and write but I don't care about anything else. I'm past the learning stage."

"You are past the stage of what, Diagne?" asked the schoolmaster, arriving with a pile of books under his arm. "Here are your books, Madame."

"Thank you, Seck."

"Can I take more of them?"

"Sure."

At this moment Gomis arrived in his van along with Joseph. "Hi, everyone. This is for your wife, Faye. It's from my mother. Father could not come to see you but he asked me to bring you his greetings."

"I'm really spoilt," said Isabelle. "Itylima's mother sends me a chicken every three days."

"We're all only talking about you … it really was quite a brawl."

Diagne intervened: "I regret not having taken part. Today Desiree asked for news of you. Previously this girl had never spoken a word to me."

"For once some girl has spoken out. I'm very pleased." It was Agnes who, arriving out of breath, had just sat on the ground. "What idea possessed you to come and live here in this wilderness?"

"I didn't imagine you'd come to visit me," replied Oumar, laughing.

"I won't speak to a pugnacious guy. I came to see Isabelle."

"Go into the kitchen then."

"Oh no! I'm staying right here. Bonjour, Maman Rokhaya. Always with her pipe," she added in French.

In their discussions they used a range of languages: Joola, Portuguese, Wolof and French. Picking up a phrase that had been left in suspense, Agbo went on: "Here every initiative is left to other people, to those who control our evolution. The only thing that Blacks do is to erect barriers between themselves, between the educated and the illiterate who think we are traitors and see us as haughty, looking down on them. All the same they are just starting to learn and they are satisfied with the crumbs of knowledge that they collect. The slowest learners are those who are the followers of Mohamed."

Now it was Joseph, the young white doctor, who was speaking. "Don't say that, doctor, you want to jump the gun too fast. We are at a moment between the two Africas. It's our job to learn from the older people the wisdom of the past and from the young ones what they want from us, although for the moment our understanding falls short of what we want. As far as I am concerned when a White and a Black suffer from the same sickness, of course I would treat them in the same way. But what I don't understand is that among you there is no desire to build a nation."

"What you say is very true, colleague," responded Agbo. "I will always be among those who refuse to accept that our country is a property purchased by the European countries; the fact that we don't care about our true value, or that of Africa, that doesn't mean…"

"It's only you who can demonstrate this value. If you underestimate yourselves it shows that Africa means nothing to you! Whereas my fathers and mothers – the toubaabs as you call us – talk about 'our colonies', but you, what do you say?"

"I am one of you only by marriage so I keep my mouth shut," said Isabelle who was bringing in the coffee pot which was giving off a pleasant aroma. She poured out the coffee, glancing at Oumar the while, for he did not much like his wife taking part in this kind of discussion.

"Then if I understand you we should all go back to our school desks? I tell you now. I refuse in advance!" said Diagne.

The schoolmaster spoke calmly: "Diagne, I have always wondered if the doctor was correct to say that you are a complete imbecile." And he added: "This coffee is very good, Madame."

"Thank you, Seck, you are the only one to congratulate me."

"Agbo never said that I was an imbecile. I may be slightly mad I admit, but…"

"Turn over the record, this is boring," replied Agnes.

"I have always said that females should never have gone to school."

"Diagne, the 'females' say that this is rubbish Diagne …. When I hear guys like you talking …. No! I know just one thing: on the pretext of not sending your daughters to school

100

you watch over them so that each of you can have three or four wives. You know very well that when they have acquired even the smallest amount of intellectual baggage it is impossible for you to force them into the path of polygamy."

Agnes spoke slowly, separating each syllable so that those listening could hear and understand exactly what she was saying. "Polygamy has existed in every nation. But you, insofar as you do not consider a woman to be a human being but as a tool to be used for your vile passions, you stick to your position. Polygamy is the strongest obstacle to development. Everything you've just said is nothing but empty words."

When she had finished speaking they did not know whether to congratulate her or not for the brutality of the words she had used. She twiddled her fingers and bent her head to one side. Since they had known her she had never spoken in this way. There was an astonished silence.

"Thank you, Agnes, for defending women."

"The girl outshines us. For that, Seck, come and give her a kiss. Although I am a Muslim I agree with her. You see sixty-year-old men marrying girls who are as young as their granddaughters."

"Faye, there's one thing I would like to know but it's rather a sensitive thing to ask," said Agbo. He hesitated, noticing that the silence had made Isabelle uncomfortable. Faye stopped rocking his chair, waiting to hear the question. The sun was sinking towards sunset. Rokhaya was scratching her right leg, her nails leaving a whitish mark on her dark skin.

"I want the opinion of ..."

Unable to continue, he pulled himself together and shifted his position. The two scars on his brow seemed to shrink showing that he was confused. Not being able to stop, he continued and said: "... of the Europeans about us?"

"Were you embarrassed on account of my wife? Don't worry. She has heard others talk about this.

For me it's very difficult to talk about it in a general way: however, from my personal point of view I can tell you what I know about it. The most pernicious people are the settlers. They say: 'There's nothing you can get from these niggers. They are bone idle. They are thieves. To make them work you have to use something like the chicotte. They make out that their life here is hell. They consider themselves to be heroes ...'"

Oumar had started rocking his chair again as he watched a bird fluttering above the stream.

"Sometimes someone asks you: 'Where did you learn French? How do you manage to speak it?' Straightaway he thinks that it's white civilisation that has made you into a person capable of reacting, seeing and even feeling, in other words it was their achievement. Others ask you: 'Are you used to our kind of food? Don't our clothes make it hard for you to walk?' When it's hot they say: 'Don't complain, you're in a hot country; your skin makes you immune to the heat. How do people live in your country?' There are also some who laugh at the sight of a black man. When a Black speaks to them they raise their eyebrows as if the words had fallen from the sky. In the cinema there are some who shift to another seat as the presence of a "sack of coal" threatens them, and as they leave they give you a look that makes you understand what they dare not say out loud; it's the same in the bus or the metro."

"Me, I'd shove my fist down their throat."

"No, Diagne," Seck intervened, "someone who runs after a donkey to kick it is as much a donkey as the donkey itself."

"Seck is right," replied Oumar. "You see, our compatriots

in Europe accept humiliation meekly. There are others who welcome you with amazing hypocrisy, announcing to their neighbours: 'Today I'm inviting my black friend.' They overwhelm you with politeness and then talk of the ignorance of your brothers subjected to slavery, or about how the Americans treat the Blacks there. In the face of these types the only thing to do is to keep quiet. But there is a minority who blot out all the bad things I have just described. These are the most acceptable: they treat you as a friend of the family. The French have taken three centuries to do what they have achieved. For us, I'm convinced that we need fifty years to overtake them."

"I don't disagree with you, Monsieur Faye, and it grieves me that people of my race behave in this way, but this racism is mostly based on ignorance."

"But no, Doctor Joseph, you see, Blacks are also racist. But in their own way."

"You don't need to like a city to live in it, but wait for the inhabitants to like you before settling there," mused the teacher who was seated between Agnes and Isabelle.

"Regardless of all the things you can say I would love to visit Europe, to go to Paris, to Rome," sighed Agnes.

"My sister, you are definitely stubborn."

Isabelle spoke kindly: "Agnes, we'll go together."

"Is that true? Are you going to go back there?"

"I really ought to see my parents from time to time."

"Why don't you go this evening then," Oumar joked.

The cool of the evening signalled that the rainy season was beginning. The tops of the trees were shrouded in mist.

The friends dispersed.

Chapter 2

They were crossing a plain which was bathed in sunshine. Then they entered a forest where the trees stood apart from one another, creating a canopy through which the light filtered. The light was as green as the surrounding leaves. Next, they came to an immense expanse of open grassland. Here instead of huge trees were multi-coloured shrubs. The heat felt heavy. Itylima walked ahead, carrying her shoes in her hand. Her bare feet hardly touched the ground. Beads of sweat, like teardrops, flowed down from the nape of her neck between her skin and the rough cotton cloth she was wearing. She looked back to see if the man was following her. Faye was wearing a hat, wiping his face and neck, his shirt sticking to his body. He looked like a hunter, with his gun slung across his shoulder. His mud-covered boots were picking up the dead leaves that were strewn all over the ground.

They were following the same path that wound its way among mango trees heavy with green fruit and then wild citrus trees which exuded an intoxicating odour. The girl increased her speed. A swarm of flies buzzed about in front of her. She broke a branch and began angrily to drive them away. Oumar did the same using his hat. Now they were on the shore of a lake, shaded by tall trees. At first sight this seemed to be a safe expanse of water, immobile and inoffensive. One could also believe, as the legend had it, that a child would be able wade through it without his knees getting wet.

But one shower of rain was enough for it to burst its banks and overflow onto the plain. Then the water would bubble tumultuously, soaking the earth, sweeping along the yellow mud, pushing against the bolder tree trunks that blocked its advance, knocking them over and carrying them off. Despite its sleepy tranquillity, older people kept away from this lake.

Next they arrived in an area with a scattering of fan palms, resembling the bars of a prison. A stranger might think he was incarcerated. Their tall trunks stood like columns at the top of which their huge leaves spread out like a fan. Hordes of frightened crows were flying around.

Faye wiped his face as he walked on. Itylima had slowed down, thinking that the man must be tired, for she assumed that Oumar was not accustomed to walking so far. Some woodpeckers were hammering the dead trees with their beaks. Other birds were chirping cheerfully amongst the dense tree trunks. Lizards were clinging to the bark of the trees, raising their small flexible heads.

After making a long detour the colour of the countryside turned dark green, as if by magic.

There was a line of dwarf palm trees, the tops of which had the appearance of a palace lawn. A light wind rustled the palms, controlling their movement as in a waltz without an orchestra. They were so closely entangled that it was impossible to see through them. Seen from below, their branches seemed to grow out from a common point as if they had been bound together. The bravest of the local people only crossed this place with apprehension: it was easy to lose one's way and it felt cold here. The humidity attracted snakes and it was a sanctuary for monkeys. There was a legend that no-one should take firewood from this place, otherwise the next baby in the family would be born disabled. But in reality this was the dwelling place of *Firandou*, the great Joola fetishist, whose domination of the spirits stretched from the source of the river to the open sea.

A serene silence reigned over everything. Guided by the girl, who was using her elbows and her arms to avoid tearing her dress, Faye followed obediently. She slid, she twisted, lifting leafy branches, plunging into this cold environment. She avoided thorns, walking lightly on tiptoe. Oumar had insisted that she put on her shoes again. A few steps further on she was taking them off again, and in the end Oumar gave in to her.

At the edge of this undergrowth where two paths met, where footsteps had long trampled the soil and where grass could no longer grow, they stopped for a rest. Oumar shared his provisions with his companion. He was seated on a huge fallen tree trunk and she on the other end of it. He looked in every direction as if he was an animal lying in wait. His dark eyes revealed that he was frightened.

A totally white rabbit jumped briskly out of the thicket and stopped in the middle of the path. The girl jumped up and cried out. With a rapid reflex, Faye took aim, his finger on the trigger. He had just enough time to see what it was. He stayed still, looking at the animal. Itylima's limbs trembled as she stared at the rabbit … and it stared back. The creature made a leap, pricked up its long ears, shook its head a little and then looked down to the ground. They both looked at each other. Then the little ball of fur turned away, moving with light hops. This performance pleased Oumar who was amusing himself greatly at the expense of the poor girl whose teeth were chattering with fear.

"Hop it," said Oumar, raising his arm to chase the animal away.

It was nearly night when they arrived at the village which was Itylima's home. Little pathways ran between the fences.

The roofs of the thatched straw huts almost touched each other. Naked pot-bellied children were running here and there. A sickly dog was barking, scampering on paws that could hardly support him. The villagers, squatting on the ground, greeted the new arrivals as they passed by. An old woman welcomed them outside a gap between the huts and led them to a shelter with branches for a roof.

It was here that Itylima's mother lived. There was just one room which served as a living room and, when it was raining, a kitchen. In the middle of the room a log of wood was burning. Its smoke made the eyes sting. Being accustomed to semi-darkness, Faye was able to see some *canaris*, clay jars of differing sizes, and some calabashes cluttering the room, and a mat on a raised area of beaten earth which served as a bed. Faye sat down on an upturned mortar, next to the bed. The deposit of smoke on the wood supporting the roof was like a thick coat of paint.

Itylima's mother was a prematurely aged woman whose body was scarred after years of working hard in the rice fields and harvesting salt from the marshes. Oumar could see her clearly. She had deep wrinkles across her face. She wore only a pagne riddled with holes and patched together. Completely wizened with age were her breasts, which dilated while she talked and then sagged again like little empty bags. She spoke Joola with this foreigner. There were no teeth left in her mouth, which made it look like a cavern which had crumbled round the edges. Although she had nothing, she insisted that Faye should be her guest. While he was talking with her mother, Itylima had vanished. She returned with a man who had a thick neck and walked clumsily. The two men shook hands. This was the future husband of the girl. With childlike naivety he did not stop laughing as he showed off his sharpened, pointed teeth. His face was exceptionally black.

After their meal the man offered to share his bed with Oumar. His hut was at the other side of the village. The smell that emanated from his body prevented Oumar from sleeping. The rays of the moon, illuminating the sleeping world, filtered through the damaged thatch of the roof and created a pattern of symmetrical lines on the man's body. In the half-light Oumar noticed how the walls of the hut were hung with dried corn cobs, horns of all sizes and the tails of animals. The bed, made of laths tied together with straps, rested on four forked posts dug into the ground. Dried hides served as a mattress and blankets. In a corner were some clay receptacles covered with twigs. After inspecting everything Oumar tried in vain to sleep. He was saying to himself: "If one day we emerge from this pit of ignorance we shall laugh at ourselves. But for now there's nothing we can do. But when we are faced with famine we will understand." Then he thought about Isabelle, wondering what she was doing all on her own at this moment. She was not at any risk, but... "If only I had thought of saying to my mother that I was going away for two days." As his thoughts were roving here and there sleep finally came to him.

The next day he was brought before His Majesty. This was a man who must have spent all his life sitting down. His waist was hidden in a mass of flesh that burst out on all sides. The most horrific sight was of his neck which had disappeared between a tiny head and an enormous belly embellished in the middle by an umbilical hernia. On closer observation Oumar wondered if this man was capable of rational thought. He was seated on a simply carved wooden chair. A loincloth, hidden in his rolls of fat, covered his nudity. Two or three steps away from him, a valet was fanning his hideous face. Two very thin men stood at his side.

Faye stopped at some distance from him with his hands

on the barrel of the gun with the butt on the ground. He said to himself: "This chessboard king is fit for nothing but butcher's meat. He takes his role seriously. When will he realise that he is just for show. A puppet, but one with no moveable joints? Yes, one day these relics should disappear." Then, as if to apologise for thinking this, he said to himself again: "Nonetheless he is one of our people."

The man on the left asked: "Why, man of the water, do you want to see our respected king?"

"I want to obtain some fields for growing rice and those who work for me will be well paid."

"That may be true, but you have inherited the waters so why do you want land?"

"Is that why you are carrying this weapon of war?" asked the man on the left whose voice sounded aggressive.

This man was completely emaciated. His body was wrapped in strips of cloth which he held up with one arm but which exposed his scrawny body. His attitude was discouraging. The top of his head was bald and it was hard to see exactly where his face began. He did not look as if he would ever laugh. He looked Faye up and down insolently before addressing him in a disagreeable tone: "Tell us, we're listening to you. What is this weapon for?"

And he took several steps towards the visitor, holding out his arm which resembled a plucked chicken's wing.

"I would like to have some men and some rice fields," Faye replied. Then he added in French, "fucking dickhead", which the king's counsellor did not understand.

"This man brings bad luck," he told the king.

Oumar was thinking: "Here's this puny specimen wanting to play tricks with me. It's important that I get what I have come for." Now he spoke out loud: "You are muddling everything up, wise man. My gun has nothing to do with what I need from you."

The counsellor groaned and, to give an impression of composure, he fiddled with the two strands of his white beard – a sign that he had dribbled a great deal when he was a child – at least that is what Oumar was thinking. He separated his hairs, then held them together, let them go, then stroked them and ruffled them. Oumar was watching this performance. This game was accompanied by extraordinary movements of his left eye, which was larger than the other one; he rolled it, looking first up, then down and then closing it; all this without the right eye moving at all. He did this to impress those present. The strength of this creature, half man, half devil, was shown in his face. He was feared in the village. Oumar began to fear that he might not succeed. He began to hate this man. Blood inflated the veins on his forehead.

What Faye had not noticed was that the king was only staring at the pearl coated butt of the gun. He decided to attack: "Your Majesty, I am a man of this country. My mother and father are well known to the silver haired old men of this area. You must distinguish between a friend and an enemy. I have not come here for any trivial reason and I don't want to disturb you for nothing. I don't have any hidden motive. I'm only asking you to help me."

"Hmm, he brings bad luck. I can see it on his forehead."

"Prove to me that I bring bad luck by putting your hand in the fire. If it doesn't burn I will return home tonight. Reply, man of great wisdom?"

"You will not get any rice fields. You would do better to go away."

Faye muttered to himself in French: "Hell, I have to make this man shut up."

"Your Majesty," he repeated, "I hear you, for I must leave tomorrow night."

"Tomorrow night!" screamed the counsellor.

A crow cawed as it flew over their heads. Faye readied his gun, taking aim at the bird. He allowed it to fly away a little and, when he judged it was at the right distance, he fired. They all saw it wheel around as it fell. Faye returned to his seat.

"I spent four years killing men. I never miss twice, and this gun doesn't reload. Do you understand that, fatty!"

The king was impressed. With difficulty he turned towards the counsellor on his right. With a great stride the man on the left came to join them. They discussed together for a moment. Then the king spoke to the visitor: "Good, you shall have what you are asking for, on condition that you give me this gun."

"It belongs to my wife, good King, but I promise that after I reach home I will send you another one in three days' time."

"No, it's this one I want," he responded, making uncoordinated gestures.

"It is impossible to agree to your demand, honourable King."

"If it belongs to your wife then it's yours."

"Only partly …"

"Why, is the wife the boss in your house? Do white women give orders to their husbands?"

Oumar could have killed him for saying this. But Itylima appeared just in time.

"Fisherman's son, you are intransigent," said one man who had not yet spoken.

"I want to please you, but I don't give away things that don't belong to me."

The girl saved the situation by swearing by her virginity that the other gun was identical to this one.

Oumar stayed two more nights in the village to organise the work.

Chapter 3

Sitting on the steps, Isabelle was on her rocking chair with a workbasket on her knees. Near her on the ground were two books. She was looking into the distance towards the garden gate near to which a lot of miscellaneous objects were piled up. The market gardeners had been leaving their things: gourds, demijohns, tools for pruning trees. Oumar had explained to her why they did this. One morning she had even surprised a woman with her child sleeping in the open air outside her door. This had amazed her. Oumar had tried to make her understand the mindset of his people. She was astonished every time. How could you make use of someone's house without having even asked them?

As she did her sewing she watched people going in and out, taking what they wanted. A woman passing by with her baby tied to her back was drawing water from the well. Isabelle was reflecting on this life which was new to her and she was making a collection of her observations. She took a deep breath as a gentle breeze brought her the sweet smell of the trees mixed with that of the water lilies. Birds were singing cheerfully. The noise of the ducks among the reeds attracted her attention. They moved gracefully in the stream, swimming away, returning, turning and plunging their heads into the water, while the moving shadows of the palm trees were reflected in the water. Some swallows had built a nest on the side of the roof from which the incessant sound of chirping could be heard.

Faye had been away for two days and nobody had come to see her. She had no fear of solitude but she did not like it. During these two days she had been busy with the henhouse and the vegetable garden. She had been along the stream to check the fish trap. There had been one catch but, not knowing what to do with it, she gave it to someone who was passing by.

She was feeling bored. Life was becoming too regular. For sure she had very much wanted to come here, and now everything around her seemed to weigh on her. The previous evening she had been playing her record player until her head was spinning. Her nerves were on edge. She felt overtaken by nostalgia for Paris. Images arose before her eyes: a spring afternoon; she was hearing on the radio about shows, theatres, cinemas, concert halls, or just the terrasse outside a brasserie on the boulevard. Poor Isabelle, how she would love to inhale the acrid smell of motor oil on asphalt, hear the hum of cars, intoxicate herself with noise and especially to see people, the crowd, the anonymous crowd on the streets of Paris. Isabelle was homesick. This exuberance of nature was starting to be too much for her. She would prefer to see a well-maintained garden with trimmed hedges and bushes in straight lines. She wanted to see department stores again, with displays of lingerie in the window. She had never before felt such a burden of loneliness. Was this just because of her husband's absence or were these feelings natural? Whatever the reason, she felt as if she was slowly going to pieces.

Suddenly alerted, Isabelle saw the looming shadow of Rokhaya. She lifted her head in amazement.

"Oh!"

"Oumar?" Rokhaya was standing with her arms dangling.

"He's in the bush," the younger woman replied having overcome her shock.

Rokhaya sat down. She was wearing a very clean bodice and her pagne, folded in squares, reached down to her ankles. Her headscarf was one she kept for big days. This garb indicated that she had come with good intentions.

As she sat down she untied a large knot, taking out her pipe and a leaf of tobacco. She ground it and tamped it down, refilling her pipe, all the time attentively watching her daughter-in-law. She had not understood what Isabelle had said. She asked again: "Oumar?"

Isabelle wondered how to tell her. Looking for a gesture that would be more explicit than words, she pointed to the woodland and moved two fingers to imitate someone walking. Rokhaya understood that her son had gone somewhere. She lit her pipe, drawing thick puffs of smoke which rose in a spiral. She leaned against the post supporting the veranda, crossing her legs. Her toenails were riddled with cracks.

The presence of the old lady put an end to Isabelle's gloom. She experienced an unexpected feeling of joy. Never before had her mother-in-law revealed herself in this way. For the first time she could really look at her at leisure. Maman Rokhaya had a small face, pitch black, and eyelids that were not prominent but well drawn and arched. She would shoot her blazing white eyes at their objective and this was doubtless why people said she had one eye bigger than the other. She was rather tall and, despite her age, her figure was still trim.

"Oncle Amadou couché?" asked Isabelle, not wishing to miss this opportunity to talk with her.

"Tousours ... malate ... Allah! Bien," she replied without moving her pipe ... and concluded in her limited French: "Papa content ... pas Oumar bow wow."

She had imitated the barking of a dog which made

114

Isabelle laugh, and she went on in French: "Oumar working, working hard, not sleeping."

"Papa … " she searched for words clicking her tongue: "Papa … pray, son pray … mama pray. Son pray … Oumar bow wow!"

Isabelle interrupted: "Dog bow wow?"

"Oumar dog," said his mother.

It was hard to keep the dialogue going. Isabelle got up and took Rokhaya by the wrist. The old lady obligingly followed. She showed her round the house from top to bottom, explaining everything through gestures. Rokhaya was pleased. She opened her tattooed black lips revealing a firm set of teeth, red from chewing kola nuts. She touched the curtains as a child would. The hairs of the hides that carpeted the floor tickled the soles of her feet. She paused on the stairs leading to the upstairs bedrooms and gazed at everything, touching each piece of furniture with the tips of her fingers.

"Bonne femme, Madame."

She would have liked to say more. She went on talking, shaking her head. Doubtless she regretted not being able to say what she wanted? Continuing the inspection, Isabelle showed her round the yard and the tree nursery. Then she showed her the irrigation work that Oumar had done. Still holding her wrist she took her to the kitchen and had her sit down while she squeezed some lemons. When the drink was ready Isabelle served it and they smiled as they drank together. The mother's laughter could be seen in her eyes and came from her heart.

For Isabelle this could be counted a victory. Life is funny sometimes: you fear to confront a problem, you hesitate, you put out feelers, you defy danger and then surprise, the problem did not really exist. Isabelle had just conquered a heart she feared she could never penetrate.

Suddenly she heard the sound of a vehicle which came to park in front of the steps. She was dismayed to see two white men get out: the branch manager of Cosono and Jacques. The old lady glanced accusingly at her daughter-in-law. Isabelle was staggered, not knowing what to do or to say.

The manager spoke politely: "We would not have come if we didn't know your husband was absent. The desire to see your house encouraged us to visit you."

"Ah, come in, gentlemen," Isabelle answered icily.

Jacques followed the manager who was looking left and right. He went on: "He has good taste, your husband; at least he's not like those greenhorns, if I could call them that, who boast about nothing."

Rokhaya got up and moved towards the door.

"Maman," cried Isabelle, running after her. She caught up with her but the old lady pushed her away and departed.

"What can I offer you?" Isabelle asked with bitterness in her voice.

"Whatever you have that quenches the thirst. But why are you running after that old negress?"

When Isabelle returned from the kitchen she glanced at Jacques. They glared at each other.

He said: "Do you like this corner of Africa?"

"I don't know any other corner. Please sit down."

"When did you get to know … your husband?"

"You're very inquisitive."

She looked the manager in the eye, saying with irony and a touch of annoyance in her voice: "Why don't you ask him?"

"Today we have come as friends, Madame," said Jacques in an unctuous tone.

"Let's come to the point," said the manager abruptly. "First of all we are well informed about plots that are being hatched here … and about everything that happens here."

"In that case calm down. Since you are well informed you must know that we do nothing wrong."

"You don't deny it?"

"I've nothing to hide. Yes, we invite friends. Does that upset you?"

"You'll see, one day they will all be sent to prison. He himself is anti-white men, though not anti-white women!"

"Would you wish to see him get involved in wrongdoing? If that day comes you would need to have just cause. But I advise you: bring it on!"

"That's enough," Jacques interjected.

"If you're not satisfied, please leave. This is my house!"

"Get it straight. She's not a tart who sleeps around and would cause trouble here!"

"No, Raoul," his colleague interrupted, "We wanted to make you understand …"

He was feigning an exaggeratedly polite tone as he spoke.

"It's that the sooner you leave this man the better it will be for us all. I am at your service."

"I shall remember that when I need to, thanks …. You're disgusting. You come here with your threats and your black-mail. Just because you want to sleep with me!"

"And you, you think nothing of sleeping with a nigger? In your place I'd be ashamed."

"And you, would you like to sleep in the place where the 'nigger' has just been? Won't the traces of the nigger offend you? He's worth a lot more than you, you load of pigs!"

He stood up and she did the same. She moved back to the wall. Her head touched the end of the gun which was hanging there. Jacques advanced lifting his arms to grab her. She evaded him by jumping to the left.

"Don't come near, I beg you!"

"When I want to have fun with a tart, I don't wear gloves. Would you prefer to be cuddled by this gorilla?"

"Leave me in peace!"

Raoul, with his wineglass in his hand, seemed to be very amused.

"What are you waiting for to catch her? Do you want a hand? Come on, beauty, give in! What's the harm? Guys are used to taking everything they can."

Jacques pursued her across the room. She barricaded herself behind the couch, but to no avail. Finally she found herself shut in the angle of two walls. He trapped her. She fought back, but each movement only made the aggressor keener.

Isabelle's clothes were getting torn, revealing her skin, copper coloured by the sun and polished by the wind, and her rounded breasts .... Seen from the opposite corner their bodies seemed as one. He rubbed against her, his thighs between hers. He bent his head forward, gasping for breath with his mouth moist and ready to kiss her. She, her teeth clamped, turned her head in all directions. The manager's amusement increased. Jacques' arousal was at a fever pitch.

"Go on, Jacques, you've got her now."

Holding her by the shoulders, Jacques knocked her down. Her skirt tore and the sight of her panties caused the man to lose all control.

"Ah, the bitch! She's bitten me!" he said, quickly letting her go.

Isabelle took advantage to free herself and ran out of the room.

"Come, Jacques. Let's go."

Isabelle went round the house and came in by the back door.

The two men climbed into the car but the Citroen had

only just started to move when a back tyre burst.

"Fuck off quick or I won't answer for my actions!" Isabelle cried, holding her gun.

"But…"

Another shot rang out.

"Wait till I finish with you, hooligans, scum of the earth…"

This anger and their surprise made the two men speechless. Isabelle shouted again: "Go away with your car, you imbeciles."

"You've punctured a tyre!"

"Oh yes! And next I'm going to count up to three. If you don't leave I shall shoot inside the engine this time, and too bad if Faye finds you here."

They knew she would carry out her threat. They started off as best they could with the car bumping along in the ruts.

Back in her bedroom, Isabelle shed tears of shame. She had heard tales about such things since the first time she had gone out with Faye but today it was just too much. She rolled on the bed. Her legs caught in the mosquito net as she tried to disentangle them . In the end, still in tears, she dropped asleep from sheer fatigue. Outside thin rain was falling.

"Do you know what time it is? I've looked for you everywhere. I thought you'd gone to the cinema."

Oumar lit the lamp. He had seen the chaos on the ground floor. Isabelle got up quickly and tearfully clung round Faye's neck. With his thumb he lifted her chin: "What's the matter with you?"

"Nothing."

"Is it my mother"

"No."

"Is it my father then?"

"No, no."

"So why these tears."

"Don't ask me anything."

He went down to the kitchen to look for something to eat. Putting his gun back in its place he noticed that one gun was missing.

"Isabelle, what happened here in my absence?" he cried, his veins swelling. He rushed up the stairs four at a time, took her in his arms and shook her.

"Speak in the name of …"

"Promise me you won't do anything."

"I want you to speak. No conditions. Everything else is my problem."

She told him everything, adding nothing, omitting nothing. He bit his lips.

"Let's go away from here, Faye."

"Where do you want us to go?"

"Let's return to France."

"Return to France," Oumar repeated, moving towards the window. "Don't think of it. I want you to understand certain things …. Before the war I knew nothing. I lived for the day, my plans only lasted each day till sunset. Then, I was mobilised. I had enemies: the Germans. I was taught to hate them and to fight them. I was taught to endure physical suffering. Whether it was raining or snowing, whether it was hot or cold we had to fight. For four years I lived side by side with men from every nation, sharing the same rations, dodging the same bullets, laughing and crying together. Then when the war ended we rejoiced and celebrated our hard fought victory. We had just won back universal liberty!"

Oumar paused and clenched his fists. Then he continued more calmly: "One day, it was a year after the victory, a man with whom I had fought together said to me: 'Without us what would have happened to you who were in the colonies?' These words on the very day of the anniversary of victory shocked me. Then I understood. I understood that we have no fatherland, that we are stateless. When others say 'our colonies' what can we say? And you want me to leave? To go where? What would I do somewhere else? I am now in my own country and if I can't make myself respected here what honour do I have? A man's dignity is not only to bear children, nor even only to wear smart clothes, it is also his country. Independently of all that, it's about you, Isabelle. You cannot forget the hunger and the privations we went through to have this house, and you want to leave it? No! It's not only a chance for my future, it's my strength and it's also yours. Wherever I shall live with you it will be the same. I'm not unaware of the humiliation and I believe I know what you can suffer. But for me, where will I find my dignity as a man? Where can I struggle for it if not in the country that gave me birth? I cannot leave and I never will. The only thing I could say to you is that you may feel free to leave.

She had moved close to him and placed her hand on his clenched fist. When he finished speaking she threw her two arms around him.

The rain was beating on the roof tiles. The anger and the bitterness had nourished them. They went to bed with no thought of dining.

Gossip about the attempted rape of 'Madame' was the season's biggest story. The news had already spread the same evening. How and by whom? Nobody ever knew. Rokhaya had returned home without saying anything and she had not returned to La Palmeraie again.

Oumar had avoided the town. He had thrown himself headlong into his new activities. He had become a farmer.

Seasonal workers had arrived. He employed five of them and God only knew how hard he would drive them!

The side streets in the township were covered with a thick layer of liquid mud. It reached half way up your legs as you waded through it. The *cailcédrats*, mahogany and other trees were infested by black and purple beetles as large as a thumb, which kids would crush with their heels. Along the roadsides and in the gardens the branches of fruit trees were cracking under the weight of their fruit. Nameless flowers were springing up everywhere. Grass was invading inside and outside the houses. Bent over their hoes in the morning, the local citizens attacked the weeds that had sprung up overnight.

Isabelle took lessons in Joola with Itylima. She knew it was the language most widely spoken locally – but at heart she would really have preferred to learn Wolof. Her choice arose from her need make herself understood by her mother-in-law. The young servant did not know why her mistress was so keen to want to speak Joola. The way the white woman pronounced the words made her laugh, the kind of laughter of which only Africans are capable and which made tears come to her eyes. Itylima had been told that white women had a preference for male servants. She was not old enough to know why, nor young enough not to know what people hesitated to say. But what was more difficult for her to understand was that in some cases they were not paying purely and simply for the job. On wash days for example 'Madame' remained beside her. They scrubbed together, spread out the cloth together and shared the same meal together in the kitchen. Itylima was not treated like a servant and she knew it. Some mornings when she was the last to get up she would find her breakfast already prepared. 'Madame' would give her underwear or dresses that she no longer wore. She took great care of them, thinking that one day she would be able to impress her fiancé.

Such was the life that the two women led during the winter season at La Palmeraie. As for the master of the house, he was in high activity mode. He was to be seen in the fields and the rice paddies where women, their legs covered with leeches, were bent down transplanting the fragile stems. Oumar encouraged them as best he could. He would give them dried fish and dried oysters. When he saw a child crying he would pick it up, rock it until it slept and then lay it down on one of the mounds of earth that were like little islands in the waters of the paddy fields. He always carried with him some leaves of tobacco, some snuff and some sweets. Each time he arrived was a moment of joy for the women. He learned about their marriage plans. He encouraged and joked with them. He knew how to appear kind and gentle. Perhaps he had even won the heart of one of the girls who were working with their pagnes rolled half-way up their thighs.

If Oumar showed friendship with the women, it was different with the men. From them he demanded more. Their old-fashioned ways of working meant they could not produce more. The sun beat down on their bare waists. Facing the sun, they were digging straight furrows. Sometimes Oumar got in line and dug a furrow himself. He was not capable of being inactive. He could be seen on the land at dawn and he was still there in the evening. People wondered if this son of fishermen had gone slightly crazy or whether someone had put a curse on him. Or maybe he might be searching for some treasure buried in the ground.

When he allowed himself a break he went fishing with his uncle, or on his own. On one occasion he spotted the trace of a manatee on the edge of the stream. For two nights he lay in wait and, when the creature appeared, grazing on the foliage which it was fond of eating, with a strong movement of his arm he plunged his harpoon into its flank and rushed in his little pirogue to pursue it. And when the animal lifted its head above the water to breathe Oumar finished it off with a blow on the head. The next day there was fresh meat in the fields and the rice paddies.

The rainy season set in. The whole of nature seemed to be painted on a dark green canvas with the sky an ultramarine blue. The rain fell, obstinate unceasing rain. The earth spewed up the water as soon as it absorbed it and the water flooded the paddy fields where flocks of aquatic birds such as marabou storks, white and grey herons, ibis and ducks were swooping down. Children were perched on the bluffs trying to protect the seedlings by throwing lumps of earth into the water. At the four corners of the fields scarecrows had been erected to scare away the monkeys, partridges and squirrels which would come to dig up the seeds.

In the bush, hunting was becoming difficult. The animals had deserted the water courses because everywhere they could find pasture and water to drink. Snakes would thread their way through the tall grass without fear. The harmless boa constrictor sloughed its skin and watched out for its meals: toads, hares and other small animals which it used for food and which had moved out of the damp places where they had sheltered during the dry season.

The strongest bush animals, despite the law that says "Eat or be eaten" could no longer easily track their prey and would come by night to the villages where there were herds of domestic animals. Hyenas caused terrible damage and some big cats got right into the pens and managed to steal oxen and cows.

Bit by bit the natural world changed colour: from dark

green to a kind of grey. The clouds were hanging onto each other and staying still for a long time in one place. Farmers were finding the nights very long. Flocks of birds emigrated eastwards. Awaiting the harvest, people indulged in their favourite games while the shopkeepers restocked with cloth, varying the colours, and piling up cheap goods to whet the appetites of the customers.

There is no relaxation in a farmer's life: sowing, weeding, struggling, then waiting for the harvest. But when he feels the satisfaction that his work has been successful, when he sees his crop ripen before his eyes and the seeds he has sown grown into tall plants, caressed by wind and watered by dew, at this moment as the night turns shapes into reality and in the distance a bluish heat rises above the blood red of the horizon and the birds slice through the air with their wings, he forgets his weariness. He might even regret not having made more effort, and pride and joy fills his heart. Yes, life, this life of a labourer, is a beautiful life.

"Oh my country, my beautiful people!" Oumar was singing as he trampled the ground.

He walked alone across fields. Who knows what he was dreaming? He stopped by a groundnut plant to straighten its leaves, he liberated a fly that had been captured by a spider, he avoided treading on a beetle. Further on he separated two stalks of millet and he propped up a corn stalk that was too heavy. He imagined he was standing before his people and, helped by the silence and solitude, he was overtaken by emotion. He was speaking and listening to the voice of his people and they were responding to him.

He had had built an enormous barn, on stilts due to the wet ground. With simple tools he had widened the stream. *Fayals*, large pirogues capable of holding ten or twelve persons, were moored side by side. Wild ivy twisted up the walls of La Palmeraie. The wide leaves of the water lilies concealed the sleeping surface of the water.

Harvest was imminent. Faye began again to visit the market to check the prices. He had budgeted for a sack of rice for Fayene each month.

One morning when he went to Fayene he surprised his mother as she was giving Isabelle a test: she had made progress in learning Joola. She had explained to her mother-in-law about the visit by the two white men. Rokhaya had believed that her daughter-in-law had a lover and this had greatly upset her. Now that she was convinced that this was not the case she relented. The subsidy that her son was paying to 'the big house' had changed her view of the white woman. Seeing that there was no alternative she developed feelings that were more maternal. But she kept one thought in the back of her mind: the only compensation she wanted was to be a grandmother. It would soon be a year since the marriage and she had not yet noticed any sign of pregnancy.

"What are you doing?" asked Faye who was standing on the threshold.

"I was just thinking," said Rokhaya in Wolof. "Your wife cannot have a child. She must come to see me."

"Have you understood what she wants, Isabelle?"

"We have been doing this for quite a while," replied Isabelle as she buttoned up her blouse.

"Well, that takes the cake! And I knew nothing about it. Aren't you frightened?"

"No. I wanted it for you."

"It's not about my life but about yours," grumbled Oumar. "Baby or no baby, I don't mind either way."

"I know that … my dear, I know."

"Why … frighten," the old lady intervened, "'Madame'

not dead."

He breathed heavily, knowing that everything was being decided without his knowledge. He scratched the back of his neck and, half consenting, he grumbled: "Okay, do as you wish ..."

"Your mother has made progress with French, and me, I've been learning Joola for a few months."

Then, turning to her mother-in-law she said in Joola: "Me, come…" and she counted three with her fingers.

"Yes," Rokhaya nodded her head.

"In three days then, mother."

Oumar pinched her cheek.

"Son of a dog. Aren't you ashamed of hurting me?"

They went away laughing. The old lady's heart sank. It was too much for her. She could not bear to see them departing without her. She said to herself: "The day they have a little one, I'll take him with me!'

La Palmeraie was bathed in sunshine. Itylima received the visitors, announcing that they were expected. The first visitor stood up as he entered, placed the book on the chair and introduced himself.

"Pierre, from Cosono."

He was dressed totally in white and was not wearing a hat.

They all took their place on the settee.

"Will you bring us something to drink, Itylima? Yes, I'm listening to you, Monsieur."

"That's it. As I knew that you had … in a word … we would like to purchase all your crop."

"And if I don't sell it?"

"I don't know what you would do with it."

"That's not the question. For the moment I'm not selling."

"Thank you," he said as the black girl put the tray down and handed him a glass. "I could be useful to you, Monsieur Faye."

"How many years have you spent in Africa, Monsieur Pierre?" asked Oumar.

"I've been here seven years. My children were born here. But not in Casamance, in Saloum."

"Tell me, at your board meetings do you envisage providing the peasant farmers with any aid?"

"We do not even discuss it."

"So, each season you buy the harvested crop and you don't care how the year has been for these poor folk? It appears that there is an agricultural college to train peasant farmers. When they leave they are not provided with anything to help them develop, and yet the needs of the country are growing all the time …"

"Excuse me. I can see what you want to say but that's none of our business. Nonetheless, school has helped you in some way."

"Wrong. It's the war that helped me."

"I will give you five francs above the current rate."

"When I do business I do it with honesty. However, I will need a pick-up truck in good condition."

"I understand. That can be arranged in two or three weeks from now."

"I have my mechanic's certificate. I know that in some places when selling to Blacks they get landed with junk."

"Trust me."

"That's not a given."

"Madame, your husband is uncompromising," said Pierre, as he was standing up.

"He has his reasons," said Isabelle, looking down.

"You'll have your truck in a fortnight. See you soon.

Monsieur, Madame."

When he left Isabelle felt worried.

"Why are you so suspicious? We're not risking anything."

"Oh, I don't know. He has a shifty look about him."

"There are good and bad guys everywhere."

He did not reply but just enjoyed a smoke. He knew why she was feeling that way.

Chapter 4

The sound of drums resonated in the cool air of the dusk. Sometimes from the north, sometimes from the south, sometimes at a rapid beat and sometimes more slowly, they seemed to answer each other. They sounded like strong voices but with no words, like vibrant musical notes which broke the silence, shook the earth and passed above the sleeping waves, embracing the rugged trunks of the giants of the forest, waking the sleeping birds on their branches.

Against their mothers' wishes children were rushing in a mob towards the town square, some carrying a bundle of straw, others a bunch of sticks. Oumar, who was taking advantage of the quiet of the evening to do his accounts, could also hear the sound.

"Isabelle, there's wrestling this evening if we want go. Then you could go and see my mother ..."

All those who were interested in this noble sport were there. A fire had been lit beneath the branches of the big kapok tree around which a great circle had formed. Passing by Fayene on the way, Oumar had brought a chair for 'Madame'. The Secks were there and with them all the usual gang.

With bare feet, wearing nothing but trousers tied up with a string or with several loincloths around their waists, Joola and Mandingo were challenging each other. They quickly came to blows. This is a brutal fight with no holds barred, where you grab hold of your adversary in any way you can.

Speed and surprise are more likely to produce victory than brute force. The light of the fire, to which fuel was constantly being added, made the sweat shine on the powerful torsos of the fighters. Their bodies were shaped like a vase with their broad shoulders and a thin waist, with a dorsal spine showing and muscles bulging from both sides of their backs. This was a new experience for Isabelle who had only ever seen these men working in the fields where they appeared to be indolent, but now she saw them transformed into superb, surprisingly agile athletes.

As soon as one of the adversaries fell down, the fight was over. Piercing cries then rang out which even drowned the sound of the drums. The winner did a few dance steps and to encourage him the women sang and clapped their hands doubly fast.

Gradually, annoyance grew among the people of other ethnic groups who had come to watch: the Balanta became more tense, the Serer more cunning, those from the south more violent. Each group was provoking the others with gestures and shouts. An open fist thrust forward indicated to the winner that he had a challenger ready to confront him. When the challenge was accepted they both advanced towards each other, swaying on their long, thin legs, collecting on the way a handful of earth which they threw in each other's faces as a sign of provocation. When they saw this the spectators cried: "*A busulu, a busulu!*" (bring him to his knees!).

After the fight they went to Fayene where Rokhaya was waiting for Isabelle. The hut where the incantation ceremony was to be held was set apart from the other buildings. The interior was gloomy: there were upturned clay pots; and the ends of pestles sticking out of the damp soil, whitened underneath from being soaked in sour milk. Outside was a pot full of water with pieces of bark floating in it; horns were scattered here and there, some red ones adorned with cowrie shells, others green with strands of animal hair.

The two women had just entered when Rokhaya let down the mat which served as a door and lit a candle. Then she asked Isabelle to undress. She herself was only dressed in a short, immaculately white pagne.

At this moment a light rustling sound could be heard from the slats that supported the roof. Now naked, Isabelle shivered. Rokhaya, holding her by the hand, walked her round the *Hames*, singing, murmuring a monotonous chant with a strangely modulated sound. Isabelle felt cold. Beneath her feet she felt the dampness of the wet soil. A sudden sharp whistling sound made her jump. Pushing out its head like the point of an arrow, a snake was slowly descending from the roof towards the face and shoulders of Rokhaya who was still chanting. Sliding from her neck to her waist, which the candlelight illuminated, the snake wound and unwound like a spiral around the old lady's body. Isabelle, half dead with fright, dared not move, fascinated by what she saw. In contrast Rokhaya showed no sign whatever of fear. Her chant had now turned into a kind of long speech. The snake, appearing to obey some secret command, rose up to face Isabelle with its forked tongue shooting out towards her.

Isabelle could no longer bear the cold glare of these grey-green eyes and an icy liquid seemed to flow right through her body. She wanted to step back but very gently Rokhaya made her stay in her place. Then she grabbed two horns that were hanging on the wall. She handed one to Isabelle and threw the other one up towards the roof where it remained suspended in the air without moving. Rokhaya then went into real trances with every movement accompanied by a plaintive song, a supplication which was sometimes more like a command, brief and hoarse. The reptile emitted a new hissing sound and the horn in the air began to move.

Isabelle had lost all notion of time. Half the night was gone; the firewood had turned to cold ashes and the ground felt cold. It was the time of night when genies visited homes to take away living souls.

Rokhaya took some water in the hollow of her hands and sprinkled it over Isabelle. The snake rose up between Isabelle's legs like rigging at the bridge of a ship. Again, led by the old lady, Isabelle had to move around the hut, stepping over the reptile which raised its head each time she passed. Finally Rokhaya gave Isabelle a beverage to drink which tasted of tree bark. She made her sit on the clay pot and examined her. At length she stroked the shivering body with her rough hands which, shown this tenderness, gradually calmed down.

Oumar, who had waited a long time outside the door, stifled a yawn when he saw her reappear.

"Well, that's about time. I'm falling asleep."

Isabelle held his arm but did not speak a word on their way home.

Three days later Faye went down with a fever. At first he felt his body shake and shiver. Next he found himself bathed in sweat. It was a violent attack of malaria. The mosquito carrying the disease must have stung him in the long grass when he was in the bush. Rokhaya was alerted. She announced that someone had cast a bad spell on her son. Where he lay, looking half dead, fetishes and animal skins were jumbled in every corner of the room. For several days Oumar was delirious. To make matters worse, Itylima had gone to her village for the circumcision ceremony. The presence of Rokhaya did not worry Isabelle but when the African doctor arrived Faye's mother emitted such loud screams that the doctor got angry and Isabelle wondered if it was really necessary for Rokhaya to stay at La Palmeraie.

At sunrise Faye felt a bit better but when evening came it was no longer possible to keep him in bed. He was very agitated and talking at the top of his voice. He was doubled up with pain as though the devil had taken possession of him. The two women took regular turns to look after the patient. Rokhaya rubbed his body with vinegar, which would briefly calm him. To drink she gave him concoctions of tamarind mixed with unknown plants. He immediately vomited and then fell asleep. Everyone was worried at the seriousness of this attack, for it had now lasted more than a month. His father came to La Palmeraie for the first time, together with some of the faithful, and they prayed to the Almighty for his recovery. Uncle Amadou had gone to look for a charlatan who confirmed the aged mother's doubts. He stated that the evil that possessed Oumar had escaped into the stream and it had to be found at any price or he would die. A few days later Amadou was seen coming back holding a strangely painted egg and he performed curious rituals with it.

However, as the days passed, Oumar was finally becoming his old self. He had grown much thinner and Isabelle was upset to see him like this. He had one last bad attack of dysentery. They wrapped him up in cloths and blankets. The corners of his lips were covered with pimples.

Finally, one morning he could be brought down into the garden.

"You've come back from far away, my dear," said Isabelle as she covered his knees with a blanket.

He did not reply. His vacant stare was directed into the distance. In the shade of the guava tree but with his wife nursing him, he was returning to life. And she reported to him all the main events that had occurred while he was ill. Itylima had departed. So had Joseph, the young white doctor, who had been summoned to Indochina and had taken the plane to Dakar the very day that Faye had his first attack. All the young regular visitors who came to La Palmeraie missed this thoughtful, serious companion. As he was to pass through Paris on his way, Isabelle had given him a letter for her parents and, as a souvenir, the jawbone of the swordfish that Faye had caught. She laughed as she told him: "That will be an amusing curio in our sitting room!"

"How long have I been lying in bed?" he asked.

"Today it makes one month and twenty days. Do you want a cigarette?"

"No thanks ... that's the first time I've been so ill; I have had several small attacks ... it's astonishing."

"I was dead with fear ... Hey, there's a letter from Louise."

"What does she say?"

"Would you like me to read you the letter?"

"Yes."

My dears,

Isabelle's last letter upset me a lot. This cursed disease must have shattered you both, him physically and you mentally. You know I love you. Don't forget that I was the witness and the accomplice of your idyll, in a word, your chaperone, and now that I know that the 'big man' has kept his word, my fraternal love has done nothing but grow. Our parents are proud of you. The young doctor who brought us this sort of beak of a fish was full of your praises. He told me how you welcome all these young people at your place. But there was one thing that shocked us. That was when he very tactfully spoke of this vile attack of which you were the victim.

Papa shut himself up for three days; and, as for your mother, I don't know if she has got over it yet.

I went to the church and lit a candle to make Oumar recover quickly. Don't laugh. I believe in it.

Regarding your mother-in-law, don't worry about her. Do you remember how mother was when you wanted to marry? Racial prejudices were slow to disappear.

It's time to leave you. I'm not complaining. I feel as if I am not really needed any more.

Let me touch your cheeks with my pink lips!
Louise

She'll always be so mischievous!"

"There's also a letter from papa. Aren't you tired?"

"No," he replied, licking his dry lips.

This letter was written in a more sober and serious style.

My dear children,

It is very nice to get your news from time to time, even if we sometimes have to worry about your health. The fever that attacked you must be a disease endemic in your country. Look after yourself properly, my little one. Listen to your mother's advice. The fact that she knows all about medicinal plants is reassuring for us. So, don't be too harsh on her. To be in favour of progress does not mean we have to renounce the old traditions.

Thank you for the present. I had a long conversation with your friend the doctor. There are things that hurt one's self-esteem. But whatever the hurt, I ask you to think carefully. Force must only be used after careful thought, otherwise we are beings with no conscience. I remember our first meeting. When you said to me: 'Do not judge me on the basis of my skin…' and you know what followed. As for you, my daughter, don't worry on our behalf. We are pleased to know you are happy, and I say with pride: 'My son-in-law is a black man.' It's not his race that makes a man, nor the colour of his skin.

In recent days your mother has had an attack of asthma. I think that maybe in your country there is a remedy for this. Faye, ask your mother.

Louise would like to visit you, but her mother is hesitant. What do you think about that, my son?

Wishing you, my dear children, our most faithful affection.

Papa.

Faye explained to his mother the contents of the two letters. Faye took them, trying to decipher the shapes that danced on the page.

"Is it true what you say?" he asked.

"Yes. If you don't believe me take them and give them to someone else to read them to you."

"They are good parents."

"By the way, I've not seen Itylima."

Isabelle told him the reason for the girl's departure. The sun was going down. The birds were coming to shelter beneath the low branches.

Isabelle asked: "Do you think women need to be circumcised?"

"No."

"Then why do they do it?"

"It's very hard for you to understand because you weren't born here."

"Did your mother undergo this operation?"

"Ask her."

"I don't dare to ... Agnes, come and advise me," she asked

137

her as she had just arrived.

"How's the patient?"

"Not too bad," replied Faye, stretching his legs.

"The last time I came … oh la, la la."

"You're looking lovely, where are you going?"

"I bought this dress at SCOA – not too expensive. Would you like one?"

"Thank you," Isabelle replied, "but tell me, why do girls get circumcised?"

"That's happening less and less."

"Did you do it?"

"No."

"And your mother?"

"Yes," replied Agnes rather irritably.

Isabelle had gone too far in her curiosity this time. A mother is sacred for Africans, especially regarding matters of intimacy.

"If this happened in France your mother would have accepted it," said Agnes.

"I was asking myself the same question."

This unexpected answer surprised Faye.

"You see this plant growing on the guava tree?"

"Yes."

"It's mistletoe. Many years ago in Europe the Druids made human sacrifices and attributed mysterious powers to mistletoe. Now they no longer do that. It's the same here. Many things die out …. Agnes what's happened to our friends?"

"Yaay Rokhaya sent them away …. The ball will be held on 14 July. On that date we can have the hall for two nights. All the young 'Casamancians' have been invited. But there's one tricky question. They don't know whether Desiree should be included. I think that's crazy. If the whole town is invited there's no reason not to invite her. What do you say about it? While I think of it, Agbo says it's a non-issue. I don't know what he means by that."

"True, it's not an issue. What are they criticising her for? For being of mixed race, having a white father and a black mother? I'll go and find her myself!"

"Thank you, my brother, you're good. I knew you'd do it."

Chapter 5

The festival was due to take place on the last two days of the week. The town was decked with flags. They were everywhere: on the roofs of houses, on fences, on boats, even on the branches of trees. The schoolchildren had been rehearsing coordinated movements for days and days. A ball was planned to close the festival. Young people had come, not only from nearby villages, Bidiona or Adéane, but also from neighbouring towns. Some who had emigrated years ago returned home for the occasion. Also there was the Jeune Casamancienne Band, popular with dancers in Dakar, Gorée and Saint-Louis. In Ziguinchor new faces could be seen at every street corner. In Boudodi, where the band was to play, the inhabitants were proud that their neighbourhood had been given this privilege.

As darkness fell, groups of men smartly dressed for the evening were strutting about as they waited for the big moment. They went from one part of town to another to present gifts which they had brought for their friends or their future wives.

As for the women, they had exchanged their weekday wrappers for shorter *taibas*, tailored jackets, which made them look like women from Guinea; and highly prized cloths known as *légos* imported from the British colonies). The braids on all their heads looked fairly similar but they varied according to the hairdresser's ideas: some were tied together in a long ponytail using *yoss*, a fibre that is dyed black; other smaller ones were tipped with rows of pearls and separated in such a way as to expose their scalp. Some women had pushed extravagance to the extreme, having one large braid from the front to the back of the head and decorated with a gold coin. Girls who had returned from Paris were dressed alike in their evening outfit – a long green dress hastily created. For them braids were no longer fashionable but their hair was carefully combed and tied with thread. They formed a group apart.

The band, on the platform, was waiting for the ball to begin. There were shouts from one table to another, news exchanged with much noise and laughter. It was going to be lively evening.

Responsibility for the running of the festival had been assigned to Diagne who was moving from place to place. He loved his role as master of ceremonies. He welcomed people courteously and had a friendly word for everyone.

"Some people are starting to sneak out. Shall I start things off?" asked the elder Gomis, the doyen of the occasion.

"Start it then."

The old man opened the floor with his wife. He was showing off the old-fashioned dance steps, to the acclamation of the younger generation. Some people who just wanted to see what was going on were jostling at the entrance. The District Officer, accompanied by his wife and some other Whites, honoured the occasion with his presence. They had been given seats near the musicians. Elderly Catholic ladies who had agreed to work as waitresses and receive a small payment did their job conscientiously. Faye, wearing black trousers and a white jacket, had just entered with Isabelle who was dressed entirely in white.

Desiree was standing in the entrance. The pearly white of her face, neck and arms seemed to float in a luminous mist. All eyes were focused on her. With a calm audacity she defied everyone. Unlike the other women with their complicated curls and locks, she had let her hair down, just brushed and glossy, and a shiny dark cloth was unfurled over her round shoulders. Her long dress with a low diamond shaped neckline revealed a gold chain and cross which was suspended and hidden between two well-formed breasts.

All three were greeted in the middle of the dance floor and were led to their table on the far side of the platform.

"My dear, you are late," said the elder Gomis.

"My carburettor broke down on the way."

"How are you, Desiree?"

"Good, Papa Gomis."

"And you Madame?"

"Not too bad."

"Everything's for the best then."

"What would you like to drink?" asked Diagne.

"Whatever is the best," said Isabelle.

Faye danced with his wife. Diagne had Desiree in his arms. He winked at Oumar as he got near him. The ambiance was good and couples formed, one after another. Over their heads the chandelier glittered. The District Officer was in discussion with the shopkeeper. One dance followed another. Whirling to the sound of the music, ten at a time the couples moved around the dance floor. Isabelle changed partners for each dance, never seeming tired. Oumar withdrew into the courtyard for a moment with Desiree; they were sitting on a bench and only the white of her dress was visible from a distance.

"You are in a pensive mood, my dear," said Faye, interrupting the heavy silence.

"I was thinking of lots of things."

"It's not always good to think too much."

Desiree was silent for a moment, then she replied: "She's very nice, your wife."

"It's good to hear you say that. Have you had any offers of marriage recently?"

The girl bent her head back and gazed at the stars, though they were shining too weakly to illuminate the night.

"Maybe there is someone who'd like to marry me but I don't want it."

"And why?"

"Won't your wife be jealous if she sees us?"

"She has no reason to worry. But you still haven't replied to my question."

"I ought not to tell you, unless someone has told you to ask such a question …. It's on account of my mother. People here don't like her and if I leave her what will happen to her? Mixed race people like us don't belong anywhere. Not to any group, and for that we suffer a lot."

"And if you loved your future husband?"

"All the more reason. He's not obliged to look after my mother, but she …"

"But look at me. I live happily with a white woman."

"You're a man."

She spoke hesitantly. "What do you care what people say," she continued. "Anyway, everyone talks about you, some with admiration, others with contempt, and these ones are more numerous. I saw you at the port on the day of the fight. Afterwards when I met Diagne, I asked him about you. I didn't dare approach you."

"Why not?"

"Perhaps because you're no longer the same."

She stopped.

"The fact of being married to a *minnediérou brancou*, a

white woman, does not make someone more or less important. I don't understand …"

She interrupted: "You are someone now. Why don't they arrest you? Others are in prison for doing less than you've done! But you are rich and respected, your wife is white. They say that this evening has been organised at your expense."

He could hear what she said despite the sound of the music in the background. For him this was all new: in the year since his return he had never cared what people could say about him and his wife. He had one weakness common to all Africans: innate in him and rooted most deeply in his being he was tormented by pride. He was sure of himself, he liked to influence those around him and that is why when this girl shared her thoughts with him he felt proud.

"Desiree," he suddenly replied, "who would you prefer as a husband, a black or a white?"

Taken by surprise and not knowing what to reply she lifted her head. Her fluttering heartbeat could not be heard due to the pervading music. Waiting for a reply, which was slow in coming, he relit his cigarette.

"I would prefer a white man."

She had spoken these words as if they had been pushed out of her by an invincible force. Oumar looked at the girl who, with her eyes shut, seemed ashamed to have had her secret dragged out of her. The arrival of Isabelle put an end to her agony.

"What are you doing there? That's really your business, but 'Monsieur' is being summoned to come inside."

"By whom?"

"The old man, Gomis."

"Let's go my dears."

They moved back inside, Faye holding hands with both of them. Isabelle lent over and whispered in his ear, "What did you say to her? She looks shattered."

As they entered the ballroom Isabelle was literally grabbed by four or five dancers.

"Excuse me, my friends but this time I'm keeping hold of what belongs to me," Oumar laughed. "Alright, Agbo, take this lady," he added, thrusting Desiree into the doctor's arms.

The couples were swept away by the waltz. Dresses were flying, revealing legs and shapely thighs. Suddenly the music stopped and the band leader announced the start of a competition for the best dancers. He introduced the members of the jury among whom were the District Officer, Gomis senior, Faye, Seck and Agnes. The band struck up again. At first there were so many taking part that it was difficult for the jury members to see who was making mistakes, but the band increased the tempo and many dropped out.

Soon only seven couples remained. After the boogie-woogie four more dropped out, exhausted. Then the samba caused one of the remaining three couples to stumble. The only ones left in the ring were Diagne with Desiree, and Isabelle who had as a partner a man who had come in with the last to be invited. Diagne was handling his partner nicely, responding impeccably to her movements. Her long dress hugged her body. Either by accident or perhaps deliberately Madame Faye and her partner were eliminated. Then there was endless cheering, clapping and drumbeats. Everybody wanted to congratulate Diagne and Desiree. At the top table a basket of flowers and bottles of perfume were presented to the happy winner.

"Now the champion must kiss his partner," announced the master of ceremonies.

All eyes were fixed on them. Desiree blushed. Diagne bowed, lowering his head. She closed her eyes and his lips touched each cheek. When she opened her eyes she noticed that Faye was watching her.

"A thousand apologies, Madame," said Isabelle's partner, "Without my clumsiness this honour would have been yours, so please consider yourself the moral victor."

He spoke fluently, gesturing as he spoke. Then he introduced himself: "Monsieur Cissé, a barrister in Dakar. At the time of your marriage to Faye, I was in Paris."

"Ah! That's why I didn't recognise you."

She found the talkative newcomer amusing.

"But Faye the Great, everyone knows him. He is as famous as …"

"Ah! Here's our magistrate, always chasing new clients," said Oumar as he joined them.

"I wouldn't want you as a client, knowing you as I do, thank you very much!"

"Don't stay too near him, my love, he will make promises of marriage, then after two months he'll say: 'You don't qualify as my ideal …" As he spoke he put his arm round his wife's shoulders.

"He's the most obnoxious human specimen with the exception of Gomis!"

The night was coming to an end, eyelids were growing heavy, the dancing lacked the verve it had at the start. The dancers no longer had the same spirit. The Whites had departed, as had Diagne. Everyone would have a chance to see each other in the course of the next day.

Outdoors, a whitish haze made the earth seem to merge with the sky; drop by drop the early morning dew dripped from the leaves.

The official ceremony took place the next day. In long processions they moved towards the port. All the local inhabitants led the way, followed by important citizens with medals hanging on their immaculate boubous. These men took their places on the platform. Rays of sunshine that were dispersing the morning mist picked out the military medals and those of the Légion d'Honneur. The Casamance River was flowing peacefully. Not a single pirogue was moving across its waters. The boats were displaying their multi-coloured flags. Only the mangroves on the opposite bank retained their usual colour and their calm.

The brass band of the Catholic mission played the Marseillaise as the District Governor arrived. He clicked his heels and made the regimental salute. Everyone copied him, some raised their hats, others stood to attention and those with a toothpick in their mouths removed it. Then a small girl dressed in white came to present a wreath of flowers to the commander who placed it at the foot of the war memorial which, as everywhere else, represented the allegory of France holding in her arms a wounded soldier. On the plinth were the words, "La France reconnaissante à ses enfants."

After the laying of the wreath, the District Officer took his place on the tribune. With their blue berets, white shirts and red belts, the children from the two schools competed in a martial procession. When they drew level with the officials they swung their arms, puffed out their skinny chests and stamped on the ground with their heels. Next came the *gardes-cercle* dressed in khaki shirts, shorts and puttees. Their cartridge pouches were not loaded.

After the procession Faye and his wife strolled from one game to another: the sack race, the greasy pole, duck races on the river, and on the quay over the water a beam coated with wax along which children had to walk to reach the ribbon that entitled them to win a prize. Only the dock workers were complaining about this day which deprived them of their work and their daily bread.

"It's really like a French fête," said Isabelle.

"Yes, near enough. Let's go."

Gomis' car dropped them at Fayene. At the sound of the motor, Rokhaya came out and spoke to her daughter-in-law: "Very solly, Madame."

"Thank you, Maman … but I'm tired."

"Your wife needs to rest and so do you," said the old lady. "We're going home."

Rokhaya took Oumar's hand and held it to her heart.

For some time after they had left she could still hear the wheezing sound of the old car.

PART THREE

Chapter 1

Clouds were returning as the hot season ended. The clear blue sky and the grey-green earth promised renewal. Trees and foliage were full of colour as though they had been freshly painted.

The end of the bad season brought the farmers back from their other distractions. Festivities were over. The fancy costumes went back to the bottom of the wooden trunk. People had spent all their money: the season had left them in debt. Their granaries were empty and now they were hoping, God willing, for a good harvest.

Faye had sold half of his produce and he hoped to sell the rest to the big companies at a high price. He took up his work again, extending his fields, increasing the number of rice paddies and even starting to cultivate cassava. He had become harsh and strict, typical of those who work the land and live off it.

Everyone rejoiced, watching the soil burst open as seedlings pushed themselves up, like the joys and sorrows of childbirth seen at ground level. Inhaling the air and drinking the dew, the seedlings were basking in the sunshine. The young men had begun to watch over these tender shoots from dawn to dusk.

But then suddenly came a day of mourning and tears. The farmers were totally distraught. All their hopes disappeared. As far as could be seen the land was bare, with no sign of growth, nothing but a dark, moving morass spreading in all directions. This destructive mass had devoured everything, the good and bad seeds. It was even attacking the roots. It was devastating everything. The delicate perfume of jasmine had given way to a dull, noxious odour. More fearsome than an epidemic, the larvae came out of the ground in myriads. In just one morning they had eaten away the product of weeks of work.

No-one had noticed the arrival of the locusts. They had doubtless come in the night to lay their evil eggs. And in the morning when the watchmen discovered the larvae there was total confusion all over the fields. Immediately the strong sound of drums announced the grim message. People came running from all directions. Some came armed with branches of trees; some arrived beating on tin cans; others had flaming wooden torches, which they dipped in palm oil; yet others were carrying shovels. They scattered across the land in all directions like sheep without a shepherd.

Oumar Faye had arranged to meet Agbo that morning. For the young doctor to cut short his working day the subject must surely be something that touched his heart. Faye heard what he had to say in a brotherly way. They went for a stroll along the edge of the market.

"Yes," said the doctor. "I went to her house … and I don't really know where this girl wants to go."

"Listen, Agbo, this girl is not typical. Try to understand.

She has many ideas about marriage …. You love her. You loved her even before I arrived. You are afraid of being rejected. But how can you be sure that she has no feelings for you? How? You've not asked her anything."

Agbo stopped and asked: "Tell me then if she has said anything about me."

"No. You see, I have never spoken to her about you, but only about what would be her ideal guy…"

"Ah," said the doctor. "And what type of guy would that be?"

"She…."

The words stuck in his throat. Oumar had just heard the drums calling, their serious tone, the rapid beats. He thought that the silence that followed meant that this was a warning of disaster.

"I'm returning to the fields. Definitely something serious has happened. We'll talk again about Desiree but first tear off this veil of fear that surrounds you."

At this he set off, running back to La Palmeraie.

Agbo remained on his own and then left to go back to the hospital. After eight years at medical school and an internship he had been posted to Casamance. He loved his work and was convinced that by choosing this career he was serving his country. He had never had a girlfriend during his internship. However, always in contact with new milieux he had learned to develop a way of observing humanity and social differences. His vocation was satisfying and, as he often said to Seck: "We have unknown strength. It's this that makes us important and if our people are not aware of us let us think of educating them."

Nevertheless, Agbo loved Desiree. He had not shared this secret with anyone, but when he had seen Oumar in conversation with her his heart had missed a beat. The doctor was one of those men who dreaded love because he put it on a pedestal. Eventually, not knowing the best way to approach the girl, he had consulted Faye.

As soon as Oumar reached the fields he realised how much damage had been caused by the locusts. He ordered trenches to be dug two feet deep and one foot wide. With branches and pieces of cloth they drove the vermin into the trenches and immediately smothered them. Oumar drew up a plan covering an area of five square kilometres. He issued orders like a general, commanding, shouting, going from village to village in his pick-up truck to recruit helpers. But the invaders still had the upper hand.

The battle lasted six days. The old folk did not know if it was worth continuing or whether to leave it to the will of the Almighty. Scorching heat was beating down from overhead, burning men's bare backs and roasting them with the white heat of a stove. At times one of them would stand up with his hand on his waist, looking grim and crestfallen, about to burst into tears. Another one was chewing, spitting out a black jet before exclaiming: "cursed little buggers", then with his jaw clenched getting on with his digging. Another, gripped with sudden anger, was starting to dance, screaming as though possessed by the devil, trampling on the swarming mass, happy to kill them with his bare feet.

The villagers continued to stamp their feet and fill the trenches. Their emaciated bodies bathed in sweat were covered in grey-black dust. Tied to the backs of their mothers, babies were instinctively raising their tiny hands to protect their little heads from the biting sunshine. Almost everyone seemed to have grown older and famine was staring them in the face ...

Worried as to how to bring this scourge to an end, the

leading men from the neighbouring villages held a meeting. Faye was the youngest present. They met just beyond the line of the trenches.

An old man with a white beard whose body was covered in wrinkles spoke: "I'm here with you and all my family in the bush. For days we have been pursuing these 'children of locusts' but the little bastards die in the daytime and are born again in the night. What are we going to do?"

They all repeated the same question, murmuring, "What are we going to do?"

"This year," another one said, "We haven't made any offerings. If we have been punished that's the reason. Let's bring out the *Cangourang*, maybe that would make some of us decide to make more effort. But let us not forget that famine is upon us." Then addressing Oumar: "You, son of the man of the waters, we thank you, since when the water threatens us we do not come to your aid. But if you have something to say we are listening to you."

Many eyes turned to him. He stood up with his hat in his hand. Some shielded their eyes with their hands from the glare of the sun.

"Thank you, honourable elders, for giving me your trust."

He spoke calmly but his pulse was beating fast. He felt hot. Beads of sweat were forming on his brow. He continued in the same vein: "I am not a stranger here. Your suffering is shared by the people. Our tears are everybody's tears and those who live on this land and are not present at this moment also depend on you. We should not love the land for what it gives us, but because it is our land. It is a mother and a wife …."

"Oh," several people exclaimed.

"I ask you to listen to me. No-one knows the value of a nut until its shell has been broken."

153

"Indeed," said the old man, crouching with his head in his hands.

Faye went on to tell them the ideas that had been maturing in him for a long time. The moment he had longed for had come.

He went on: "I've been with you since that first morning, digging and working at your side. If we follow the plan we shall succeed in time and crush these children of evil. Some young people are going to ask for help from those not yet affected. They will lend us their strength and that is what we need. Making offerings will do nothing for us. These bastards grow bigger every day and become ever more voracious. The growing season is already upon us; either we kill these vermin or they will kill us. We shall have no rest: we must be there day and night. We will light fires twenty feet apart. Keep that firmly in mind: our lives and those of our families depend on it. You don't want to see your herds collapse nor to watch the slow agony of your children. No, you don't, do you? Let's get a move on then as we are only prattling like girls around a well. As for me, I'm going back to town to see what I can do …"

"Why don't you give us some seeds since you still have some?" someone asked.

"It's true I still have some. But you have no more brains than an old woman. Wherever will you sow them?"

There was a murmur of approval.

"We will do what you have said. If you can bring us something to eat … God will pay you," said the old man with a white beard.

"I'll do whatever I can, but quick action is needed. Also, bring out the Cangourang if you believe in it!"

The old man gave Oumar a long handshake. His look said much more than his words.

Faye went off to the Residence. This was in the centre of the European colony. The guards wanted to prevent him from entering but he climbed quickly up the steps. His footsteps resounded on the shiny floor tiles of the main hall. He raised his eyes to look around at this "house" on which thousands of people like him were dependent. The Residence was at the same time a town hall, a chamber of commerce and a magistrate's court.

Faye was thinking: "None of these pen pushers will move their butt from their chair to help us out of this bad situation. Yet it's the produce from this land that provides their well-being. I could live for a hundred years just to see the villagers fix for themselves for once the price of their labour."

Suddenly he saw Desiree in front of him. She worked as a secretary at the Residence.

"Is the administrator there?"

"Yes, but I have to ask if he can see you. He has Raoul with him... What's going on in the countryside? It seems that the locusts have devoured everything."

"Go and tell him I'm here."

He followed on the heels of the girl and when she opened the door and he heard the words, "Come in" he put himself between her and the door, pushed the flap and entered. Desiree stared at him wide-eyed.

"It's okay," said the administrator, "I had said that nobody should disturb me."

He took off his shell-rimmed spectacles.

Faye looked around, inspecting the office. Raoul and he looked each other up and down. Oumar clenched his fist. He felt the blood rushing to his face.

"Have a seat," said the administrator, and he went on: "I know why you have come. It's about the locusts. We were just speaking about this before you arrived. It's very good that you have come. You are coming straight from the bush, aren't you?"

"Yes."

His fingers stained with oil touched the varnished mahogany desk on which stood a bottle of Pernod and two half-empty glasses. The office was spacious and, as in the hall, everything was neat and clean.

"Well, tell us how far you have got?"

The administrator paused, putting his elbows on the table. Faye was disconcerted "He really doesn't care about me, I'm just an imbecile," he murmured, and out loud he said: "I've come to seek help."

"But how far have the farmers got with it?" asked Raoul, settling comfortably in his leather armchair.

"Monsieur l'Administrateur," Faye began, searching for the words, when I left from here to go to France you were not here. Nor was Raoul, he was in Upper Volta. You don't know the people here very well. For the last week and a half we have been trying to finish off these locusts and we are not yet in control of our fields. You ask me how far we have got. That's truly disappointing! I am going to give you a little account of what I have witnessed. You have never been present at a trial where the accused has not stolen anything but has simply been unable to repay the seeds he has borrowed in order to pay his tax. He is exposed in a public place when the sun is at its zenith. He has nothing on but a loincloth. He has been given nothing to drink or eat. He is guarded by soldiers. The whole village is there. All the members of his family are in the front row. It's not a pretty sight. The pain is not only physical, it's moral too. And now you are asking how far we have got. Whether the harvest is good or bad we have to pay the tax. But how can we pay the tax if we are not protected? And Raoul too is waiting for the harvest. He's a trader."

"Yes, yes, okay," the administrator interrupted. "For the moment there is nothing I can do, I am sorry."

"Ask for an airplane to spread insecticide."

Raoul intervened: "Are you thinking what you are saying?"

"I'm not talking to you," Faye shouted. "I see that the suffering of the villagers does not concern the administration. On my way here people were saying, 'Useless to go and see the "Manso". He won't do anything!'"

"Who said that?" asked the 'Manso'.

"I am not a reporter."

"Go. I'll see what I can do and if I find nothing I'll send some detainees as reinforcements."

"Thank you nonetheless," said Oumar.

And he departed after having stared at Raoul with hate in his eyes.

In the secretary's office he found himself face to face with Jacques. He grabbed him, stuck his flat nose in the white man's face and before the man had got over his shock he punched both sides of his head, causing him to fall on the floor of the girl's office.

"It's not worth your while waiting," said Faye.

Then he quickly went off to his pick-up truck. Desiree was waiting for him on the seat.

"What are you doing there?"

"I've finished at the office. Take me home."

"But you live at the other side of the town!"

Without replying she took his arm, making herself very small. He bit his lips.

"It's okay," he said and drove off.

"How's your wife?" Desiree asked.

"I've not been home for ten days."

"Oh, the poor woman," she said with pity in her voice.

157

Then, changing her tone. "What you did there was not good. If I had a husband like … I wouldn't leave him out of my sight for a second!"

They drove down the main road which went through the market and along the bank of the Casamance River. Faye dropped the girl at the entrance to Boududi.

"Shall I see you?" she asked.

"When you come to my place."

"My mother has been asking about you since the night of the ball. I don't meet the group any more. You want to know why?"

"Another time."

"When?"

"When you like, at my place …. No, I'll come and see your mother."

Turning abruptly he almost knocked her over. 'She's crazy, this girl,' he said to himself. He wiped the sweat off his brow with his forearm. He felt the same sensation he experienced each time he was with Desiree: he felt overcome by a wave of warmth. As he was narrowly avoiding a child who was crossing the road he brushed against the wall of the office of Cosono. The kids were screaming as he speeded up past Fayene and arrived at La Palmeraie. Isabelle was very surprised to see him approach from this side of the town. While he has been away her pregnancy had caused her to be nervous and sullen. The return of her husband brought her some cheer.

"Why, you have come via Santhiaba?"

"Yes, I'm coming from the Residence, then I bought three bags of biscuits and now I'm going to have a bath."

"Meanwhile I'm going to cook some food. By the way, Pierre came but he did not mention the object of his visit. And Agbo was here yesterday evening."

Oumar yawned.

Then he went to pump the water and he filled the tub. His eyelids were swollen from lack of sleep. He plunged into the water and was soon dozing as he scrubbed himself. A thick layer of soapy grime was floating on the surface of the water. He got out and dried himself quickly. Isabelle brought the meal into the living room. Wrapped in his bathrobe, Faye swallowed a few mouthfuls.

"But where's Itylima?"

"With your mother out in the country, since this morning. I couldn't understand very well what they were saying but I suppose it was something to do with me.

Unable to stop yawning, Oumar lay down on the couch.

"It doesn't matter. My mother knew the … the bush well before I was born. What can she do in the countryside?... Good, wake me in an hour. I have to go out again."

"You're not going to sleep here again tonight?"

"Again? Are you reproaching me?" he said, returning to the back of the couch.

He tried to go on talking. "I have to go there. I don't know when I shall come back …"

He stretched out and fell asleep instantly, overwhelmed by tiredness.

Isabelle was standing and watching him. Her stock of patience was diminishing day by day. But seeing him like this she understood how totally exhausted he was. She prepared clean clothes which she carefully laid at the foot of the couch.

Chapter 2

The appearance of the Cangourang was effective. No-one stayed in their hut pretending to be ill. Dressed entirely in red, the creature did not pass by unnoticed. It rummaged through the huts and the grain stores. Those who were inclined to do nothing were forced in public to correct their behaviour. Redoubling their ardour the people beat the ground without respite with the threat of the Cangourang's two swords hanging over their heads. It screamed as it went from group to group followed by its escort which it subjected to a rough discipline. It made people bend down and crawl over thorns as it walked all over them, raining them with blows. It had no fear of blood. More rapid than a hare, it could – according to the locals – fly. It hated to see the colour red, although it was red itself from head to toe. Nobody dared wear this colour in its presence.

After some weeks the process of disinfection came to an end. Those who handled the *kadiandou*, the *kuco* or the *dramba* were all present. The detainees were the happiest, despite the chains around their feet, as they could now have news of their families.

Finally, the last trench was filled. Only the squeaking of the cicadas disturbed the silence that had now returned. All that was left was a vast devastated area. Faye called everyone together.

"Now that everyone is returning home I can give seeds to those who want some."

"How much does each barrel produce? And how much shall we have to pay?"

"Nothing," he replied.

"You're crazy! The men with red ears are richer than you but they won't lend anything that does not bring them a profit … but you want a nail for a nail. I swear by my ancestors I've never seen someone from the city as crazy as you."

"That's perhaps because you have never travelled very far. For me land is everything. But you, you do not know its true value. Yes, your sons … they will know. I am lending you the seeds only on condition that you sell your harvest to me and to no-one else. I ask no more than that."

"And if the harvest is not good how will we pay you? We are already in debt ..."

"I will lose my profit but I will stick with you."

The villagers took a long time consulting each other. Then the old man spoke again.

"We are with you! When will you give us the seeds?"

"Tomorrow morning. We have to act quickly. Time is pressing."

Then someone in the crowd asked him: "Me, I have two big families. Can I have two barrels?"

"No, you'll get the same as everybody else. However, I can give you some advice. Bring the two families together."

Everyone laughed. The old man went with Oumar to his truck where he presented him with a tiger hair amulet.

"Keep it carefully. It came to me from my father who had it from his father. God be with you, you are a good son."

"Thank you. Don't forget to send a young man tomorrow."

But the man, who was advanced in years, struggled to find the right words. "There are very many of us."

"You shall have two then."

"May God watch over you!"

"Amen," he said as he left the old man.

After all this he took charge of the prisoners whose chains made walking difficult for them. The road was in a lamentable condition: the first rains had created channels where the 'forced labourers' had slaved away during the dry season. They met some women who were returning from the market. Faye greeted them, waving at them through the window. They responded with cheerful cries and their voices echoed loudly. The guard sitting beside him took note of his behaviour.

"I'm from here and I love the country," he replied.

"What you are doing is worrying."

"And why?"

"I don't know, but if a young man is too well known it can bring bad luck."

"If I die no-one will complain, apart from my mother and my wife. Anyway, I don't want to die. How many years of service have you done now?"

"Twenty years," the guard replied.

"I don't want to die for that," he repeated.

"I don't understand …"

"I've done four years and I'm sick and I'm tired of it."

The sun hid behind a threatening cloud. Faye deposited his load outside the police station. The iron-grey sky weighed down, heavy as a lid on a cooking pot. Oumar parked the truck, opened the door and found Isabelle sitting on the couch.

He mocked her kindly: "Are you sitting or lying down?"

"Sitting," she replied, knitting her brows.

"Hard to tell."

"But you're coming from town?"

"Yes, I had prisoners to take back."

"My tummy makes me frightened at times," she said,

changing the subject.

"There are days when I wonder what you've been able to eat."

She threw a cushion at his face.

Oumar held his wife's hand. The size of her stomach was alarming. Although Isabelle was dressed in a very loose outfit it failed to conceal her condition.

"Perhaps I took too much of what your mother gave me. Tell me, what are you doing this evening?"

"I'd really love to go fishing."

"Oh!" she said disapprovingly.

"You want me to stay?"

"Yes, we are the happiest people on earth and I don't complain about my husband."

"On the other hand I do complain about my wife. She smokes my cigarettes."

"I don't smoke any more, with this bitter mixture that I drink every morning. Just thinking about it makes me feel sick."

"At least it costs me nothing."

"You miser!"

"And so much the better for it."

"Do you remember our attic room at the hotel? You said to me that one day we'd have a house of our own. You kept your word. Now I'm frightened that you don't love me any more."

She patted her tummy with her hand.

"You can be silly sometimes."

"Which do you prefer? A boy or a girl?"

"I prefer their mother …."

Their conversation ended with the arrival of Rokhaya. She came every day to get news of 'Madame' and to bring other prescriptions. It was going well for Isabelle and the old lady did not stay long at La Palmeraie. On the doorstep she said to Oumar: "Your father is asking for you, my son. He wants to see you this evening."

"Okay, I'll go at sunset."

"Marcher, ptit, ptit, coucher pas bon, fatigue ... malade," she said to Isabelle, clutching her waist.

"Faye, I didn't understand that."

"She says you should walk instead of resting all the time, which is not good for your back and makes you tired."

He was translating the old lady's words while mocking his wife.

"I'm not resting," she said with vehemence. "What a mother! What a son! And what if we go with her into the bush?"

"Not with me you won't."

"Why not?"

"There are things that concern women and not men, that's the custom here. But we're going to the cinema."

"In my condition?"

"What does that matter?"

Rain fell all that afternoon and continued until the following morning.

At dawn the day broke marvellously with brilliant winter light and not too hot. The farmers had arrived, some on foot, some in pirogues. Itylima welcomed them with a full pot of kinkilibaa. Oumar received them with a kind word for each one. Isabelle, sitting on a stool, made a note of their names and their villages while her husband weighed the seeds: rice, millet, maize and groundnuts. The distribution got busier just as the sun was rising. From early morning they had been working tirelessly. Isabelle, despite her condition, did not feel too tired. However, wind blowing from the nearby forest carried with it a smell of rotting leaves that made her feel nauseous.

"Can we stop work for a bit," she said.

"Are you feeling tired? Have a rest."

"It's nothing. It will pass."

They started to work again, but Isabelle could not continue and her husband had to move her beneath the veranda to shelter from the sun and the wind.

Her voice was sad. "I feel better here. I'm sorry not to be able to help, my dear."

"Itylima and I will finish it."

He went on weighing and recording until the time the sun was high in the sky. He was hungry but he could only see faces turning to him which seemed to implore him to help them. The villagers were squatting in their usual way with their heads in their hands. Faye called them, handed them their seeds and shook their hands as they left, asking about their families and this and that. He found a kind word for each of them. Suddenly he was surprised to see his mother beside them.

"Why, mother, are you there? Have you been here long?"

"No," she replied.

She watched her son. All those present had come from their villages for him. She remembered the time he returned. He had wanted to be a labourer and that is what he now was.

"How are things at the big house?" Oumar asked.

"Good, thanks be to God. But yesterday you did not come to see your father."

"It was raining …. Have you seen Isabelle?"

"Yes. But I don't understand. Toubaab women seem to be very strong and yet they are more fragile than a drop of dew on a cassava leaf. Perhaps they are not like us black women?"

"Why do you say that? Women are all alike."

"She isn't. I'm worried that she might not be able to give birth in the normal way."

"You said nothing to her?"

"No, no," she said, moving close to Faye who had stopped registering the name of a man from Marsassoum.

"You should say nothing to her. That is why we have no children. It's since …"

"What do you want with a wife who can't have children?"

"Mother, it's you saying that … and it's you who … that night …"

Rokhaya did not wait for him to finish. She withdrew into the house.

Oumar lit a cigarette which gave him a feeling of well-being, when all of a sudden he was gripped by a fear of some disaster. He remembered the words of the doctor at the time of their marriage: 'Your wife will not be able to have a child without risking her life, for she has very narrow hips. Be warned!' He was sitting with his head down. He had forgotten about the villagers. Someone coughed to attract his attention. He picked up a handful of soil. It was black and moist. He tasted it.

"Is it sweet?" someone asked. It was Pierre who was just arriving.

"I've never tasted anything more delicious. It always retains its flavour."

At the sight of the white man all the villagers stood up and removed their hats as a sign of respect. Faye looked at his people and at the man and then shook his head.

"Don't get upset about a small thing. It will take many years to get over this inferiority complex," said the young white man. "I've come several times but you were in the bush."

"Just now I can't talk business, but nonetheless while you

are waiting you can be useful to me."

"No problem."

"Take this notebook. Write down all the names as I read them out."

And Pierre helped him with as much enthusiasm as he would have shown if it was his own business. Three hours later nobody was left and the barn was empty.

They went back into the house.

"To what do I owe the honour of this visit?" Faye asked. "Itylima, bring us something to drink."

"Well, you see," said Pierre as he sat down. "You know better than me that the damage caused by the locusts is considerable and puts the next harvest at risk; and then there are some …"

"Blacks," Faye interjected, seeing Pierre embarrassed as to whether to say 'Blacks' or 'niggers'.

"… Yes, Blacks who owe us money, and with no harvest we won't be reimbursed. If you have any seeds left, sell them to us."

"This is what I have left, nothing at all! And if I did have some left you wouldn't be the one to get them …. When this scourge had to be overcome no help came from your side. The life of these farmers is of no concern to you …. But when your interests are threatened what do you do? I saw your boss one day at the Residence during the time the locusts were here. When will you understand that you are no longer men whom we fear, that your prestige is in decline? You cannot fool us for ever."

"I'm not to blame for the things you are criticising me for, but if you are determined to continue competing with us you will be the loser, despite all the tales I'm told about your mother."

"I don't want to compete with you, I just want to struggle.

If I fail at the start it does not matter; those who come after me will stand up to you until the time you will sit at the same table as equals."

Pierre did not reply. Isabelle came down the stairs and nodded a greeting. Her face showed signs of fatigue.

"My good wishes, Madame. Things don't seem to be going very well? It's often the case. It was a similar story for my dear wife."

"Where is your wife?" Faye asked.

"She died in labour."

"Oh, forgive me."

"You couldn't have known .... You're right, you have to have an aim in life, otherwise you lose interest in it."

He finished his drink with one gulp. His expression seemed to harden.

"Good-bye, Madame. Faye, can you come with me to the way out by the palm trees?"

Oumar followed him. This confidence had brought them closer. As they reached the edge of the woodland Pierre said to Faye: "Keep your thoughts to yourself. You are making more enemies than friends. Your fellow countrymen are not what you would like them to be. I understand everything you've told me. It's the truth, but what can I do? The burden is too heavy for your shoulders .... As for your wife, keep a close eye on her. She's in a worse condition than she looks. That's all I have to say to you .... But yes, one more thing. I love Africa."

He added nothing further and he stepped up to the ridge. Oumar saw him disappear in the dust thrown up by his car.

When Isabelle and Oumar went out the night was black. Only the stars were shining. Here and there toads were croaking at each other. When they arrived at Fayene they found the aged

Moussa at prayer, telling the beads of his rosary. He shook first his right hand then his left to drive away the mosquitoes that were buzzing in his ears.

"*Assalamalec.*" Faye greeted him as he entered the courtyard.

"Oua aleck Salam," the old man replied.

Faye went around all the rooms to ask for everyone's news. Seynabou invited Isabelle into her room.

"Why did you not send her to her parents?" asked Moussa the moment he was alone with his son.

"She's my wife."

"I did not ask you to come to talk about her. This is what it's about. For a very long time, before your return, I had dreams, and in those dreams I was called to go to the Kaàba …. It's the desire of every Muslim to visit the Holy City. I can satisfy this desire this year thanks to God, to his prophet and thanks to you …"

"Father, I don't quite understand," Oumar interrupted.

"Let me finish speaking. All the men of my age have been there once or several times, but me never. That's why I asked you to come. As you know, your grandmother is dead, may God have pity on her and grant her his holy protection.

"Amen," said his son, wondering what his father wanted to say about it.

"… Rightfully this house should come to you through your mother, but I have leased it out for thirty years."

"Up to now nothing has been said to me on this subject. How can you appropriate property which does not belong to you and without warning me? When I needed money I could turn to my mother. Now what do I do? I need some."

"I am your father. My needs have to be met before yours!"

Oumar nodded and said nothing. He knew that his father

was right and that he who was not yet thirty he had no choice but to obey. Among his beautiful people the man was still in charge.

"After a long silence his father replied: "God will pay you. You do not seem to be rejoicing about of my departure to the holy places."

"I…"

Oumar stopped himself in time so as to say nothing that would upset his father and he changed his tone: "I am very pleased that you are going, since that is your wish."

"You too, you could go next year after the harvest insh'Allah."

"I shall never go there!… God is everywhere, in ourselves, on the earth which he has created, in the sky, in the water that irrigates our land, in the sun that ripens our crops …. I won't go to this place where you have to pay for every-thing, even for the shade of the trees which belong to nobody unless it's the sun. Apart from that don't let's talk about it."

"What you are saying is beyond me. It's not good to try to understand everything. You have just spoken like an atheist. Due to the fact that you stayed for a long time in Tougueul you have become a lost soul on the road to God."

When Moussa finished, his son thought to himself: "And you, when you enter paradise, close the door, double lock it and swallow the key." Faye knew why his father had called him. It is written in the holy book: 'Do not travel to Mecca without a clear conscience'. God himself has said: "I can pardon any wrong that you do to me, but any wrongs you do to yourself, it's only you who can wash them away."

"Papa," said Faye again. "I believe in God and fear him. When I am alone my mind is filled with something very large. I know that God must exist …. Sincerely, father." He lowered his voice. "Sincerely, it's good that you are making this pilgrimage. I am just asking you one thing. Oh, it doesn't cost a great deal. Look at all the countries you will be passing through, observe well the people that God has placed on your route. Don't forget in your haste to lift your eyes to take a look at the houses and the mosques. Then, my father, you will notice something. All these things were built by the hands of men. There was a famous toubaab who said: 'Man is God's conscience'. And I find he was right."

"Son, may God pardon you for your words. It is Satan that inspires them!"

"After your departure who will look after the house?" Oumar asked again.

"You are here and your business is going well, thanks be to God."

"Have a good and peaceful night," said the young man, for he could not bear to hear anything more.

He went to find his mother who stood up when she saw him enter. He asked her: "Why have you never spoken to me about the inheritance?"

"Your father didn't want me to. He is right to go to Mecca. I hope that you too will go."

"No, mother, I don't think so. I don't need to go to paradise. I want my paradise here," he said, taking his wife by the hand.

And they departed into the night.

Chapter 3

Unceasingly the rain was falling. Plants were regaining their vitality and colour; they were spreading everywhere. Men had to fight back against nature to protect the land they had cultivated. Oumar, as in the previous year, was making frequent visits to the fields. His popularity had spread beyond the limits of the local district. His informality, his humility and his patience when he talked with the villagers had added to his fame. But his character was becoming more and more cold. His passion for the land was causing his heart to harden. His project was maturing but each day his universe was shrinking. It was like an illness that was gnawing at him. He refused to confide in anyone.

Rokhaya had chosen to settle at La Palmeraie and you could smell her tobacco in every room. During the month of fasting the children from Fayene came to do the cooking at the 'little house' (so-called in relation to Fayene where the old folk lived). For them, the two households were as one and there was a great deal of activity there. They even spent the night there sometimes. The day when the fast ended – the *korité* (Eid al-Fitr) – they were reluctant to leave because 'Madame' looked after them well. And also they were not often scolded.

As for the imam, Moussa Faye, he left a few days after the korité to visit the tomb of his prophet. And that was a great day. All the disciples of this pilgrim had come to be with him. Eyes were shining with envy on every face. They had not slept all night. They were chuckling with pleasure, searching the corners of their wrappers, calculating to see how many coins they could find to send to Medina. They had visions of the paved roads enveloped by bluish smoke leading towards the Kaaba. They reminded each other of the combats fought by the disciples against the idolaters to spread the true faith, the unique and real faith. Oh, it was with regret that they evoked the time long past when, led by the revered Mamadou Rasôlilâh, they expelled unbelievers from the mosques … oh, how sweet it was to fight for one's ideals, to know that one was taking action for the benefit of the Almighty! Today they did not have the luck to do this. All that was left for them to do was to die of envy to step into those sacred places. This journey was the high point in their miserable existence. They were jealous of Moussa but at the same time they rejoiced that the pilgrim was a man of their parish. Each of them asked him to bring a souvenir: water from the Zam-Zam well, a ring, a turban, a pair of slippers …

It was at this time that Isabelle and her mother-in-law ended up getting to know each other better. Rokhaya had suddenly discovered a true fondness for her daughter-in-law. The child that the young woman was bearing had become a real part of herself. Superstitious, the old lady watched over her and each time the sun shone they would go out together into the forest. She taught the white woman the thousand and one traditions and recipes she knew. This is how Isabelle learned the secrets of plants: which leaves cured kidney problems; or those that cured stomach ache. She learned how to recognise the trace of a chameleon on a fruit; about the evidence left by a snake; the route abandoned by ants. She also knew how to differentiate the whistle of a cicada from that of a boa constrictor; to detect the holes in large trees where parrots lay their eggs; to dig up yams; to distinguish which roots are poisonous and which are good for healing a cut; to find guinea fowls' eggs; and to hide from monkeys (which would prevent her baby looking like one). In this way nights followed days and days followed nights in the long chain of life.

The club was at the centre of the European colony: it was a huge, brick-built bungalow with steps surrounding it. Its red tiled roof was sheltered by the leaves of coconut palms. Encircling the whole place was a large garden containing many different flowers with pathways covered with small shells. The whole place was designed to ease the life of white people during their stay in Africa. On the other side of the garden were two double tennis courts, a volleyball pitch and another one for basketball. A few steps led up to the veranda where sun loungers were lined up like hospital beds. The ground was a pattern of yellow, black and white squares.

In the interior the bar served as a saloon and smoking room when it rained. The bar itself was made of bamboo stalks – the only 'exotic' item in this tropical semi-palace. Hanging on the yellow and black walls were posters advertising tourist attractions in France. At the end of the bar there was a record player on a stool and, to complete the furnishings, there were tables for ping pong and billiards.

At the end of the day the Europeans would meet each other here. There were about thirty of them in the town. Three quarters of them were traders, and one quarter colonial civil servants. Winter was the hardest season for them. The long days of rain deepened their nostalgia for their home climate and made them bitter and apathetic. They sat by the dripping wet foliage dreaming about places in France; of a garden fête under a blue sky…and the longer the rains lasted the stronger the dreams grew. They did not express their feelings publicly. They kept their thoughts to themselves.

On occasion one of them, unable to stand it, pretended to be sick so that he could be repatriated. These 'illnesses' mainly affected the civil servants. The traders had other concerns. For them the rainy season was the time for finalising sales and making new bids. These offers were very important to them. They knew the psychology of the black peasant farmers and knew that the loans they agreed to were seen as 'kindness'. They also knew the risks they ran and as a result they insisted on guarantees. The local people attached little importance to this business in itself: they mainly saw it as a chance to have contact with the big white traders. They found these 'grands blancs' to be good, while the less important 'petits blancs' were bad. They were unaware that the small ones were often just following the orders of the big ones. In this way two worlds that did not understand each other were co-existing on the same land, experiencing the same seasons but they were unable to work together.

Pierre was soaking wet as he entered the bar. He shook his head and ran his fingers through his wet hair before greeting three men who were playing a card game. The black barman wearing a white jacket gave him a broad smile. The light of the lamps reflected on his forehead.

"They are waiting for you behind there," he said.

"Give me a beer first."

He emptied his glass in two gulps and made his way to the door behind a curtain. 'Behind' was the conference room. A table surrounded by chairs almost filled the room. Four men were already there, each one from a town in the province. These were the 'big men' of Casamance. Pierre sat next to the one who seemed to be chairing the meeting, a bald man with large bags under his eyes.

"As I was saying," said the bald man, twiddling a pen between his fingers, "this year I visited the farms twice. If at first we were pessimistic, there is no longer reason to be so. I recognise that this harvest will not be like last year's but we shall survive – perhaps by a narrow margin – and I don't think we shall lose money. Let's wait to know the price per hundredweight."

"Do you think that if the natives pay what they owe us they will have anything left to sell?" asked the one sitting on his left.

"Let's get our income back. Otherwise let's wait and see."

"Agreed, but don't forget that our income does not only come from the interest on the debts but on what the natives buy from us. We must face facts. Manufactured goods must be sold during the trading period. If we restock our goods during this period it's not to offer them on credit terms as we are now lending on the added value of the last harvest. Then what's left for us in the future."

These words produced a gentle murmur of approval. The speaker looked up. He had hit the nail on the head.

He continued: "It's four weeks until the harvest and we need to look into another problem, which, in my opinion, requires all our attention. I'm talking about this young nigger married this white bitch! Last year he trespassed on our patch. If I believe what people are saying, this time the farmers are prepared to sell him their harvest …. You see what that means …. Nicolas, I gave you carte blanche to get us information about his past history in France."

Nicolas, a small stocky man with a pug nose, took a paper from his brief case and unfolded it.

"The information on this man is good," he said. "He fought courageously in the war. He was decorated, demobilised at Lille where his *marraine de guerre* lived, a middle aged widow whose husband had died in the resistance. This woman is a member of the Communist Party. Oumar Faye left Lille to work for Citroen in Paris. He joined the CGT trade union and took a course in mechanics. He got to know Isabelle at the homes of left-wing friends. He went abroad for all his holidays and visited Germany and Austria. His political activities are not known, but some information received make it clear that he is anti-French. His wife's parents belong to no church. A year after his marriage he arrived here; they had altogether half a million francs in capital. Despite all the expenditure he has made, approximately half this amount still remains. In fact he should really have nothing left. Where does he get his money from? I've not been able to find out. They only receive letters from his wife's parents. Oumar has a mistress, Desiree Séverin, the mixed-race girl."

"Well, well, well, that's exciting." Raoul rubbed his hands. "We can see he has subversive ideas. There's no doubt he is a bolshevist. The young people are conspiring at his house. But on this subject Pierre is going to be able to tell us what he knows."

Pierre had not opened his mouth since he came into the room. He knew the hold that Raoul had over his colleagues. For them any competition was intolerable. Sure, they did not represent the law but they had power. Since he had been dealing with the Blacks as their agent, he knew them well.

"Oh, me," he said to break his silence, "I don't know a great deal about him. I went to his place on business. He bought a pick-up truck from me. I'm not interested in his private life."

This unexpected response drew everyone's attention to him.

Nicolas intervened: "Another thing. At the beginning of the season Faye received prospectuses on river navigation and catalogues of different models of ploughs. At his home there are Marxist books. Some of these are banned here. I think it won't be difficult to collar him. Faye is too cunning for a black but not smart enough to be a White."

"We are not the authorities," said the man sitting at Pierre's right, scratching his beard. "As I see it we can do nothing against him, at least not directly. The best thing to do is to gain the confidence of certain individuals to set against him."

This proposition seemed to please them judging by the nodding of heads that welcomed it.

"May I say a word?" asked Pierre.

"Yes."

"We are showing our true colours. Just one man is blocking us. Imagine that in future there could be thousands of them! For some years I have been moving from colony to colony. Everywhere I have seen by and large the same desire of young Africans…. We are more accustomed to the old Africans who take no notice of our activities. These old folk are on the way out and this is what you must understand. It's no longer enough to lay down laws, which are not really laws anyway. If you don't want to see what is happening around you, if you are too proud to change direction you've not got much time to do it and difficulties will emerge on your way, one after another. Do you know what these young people call us? They call us 'the ogres'".

"That's enough," cried the chairman. "You're talking nonsense."

"Let me finish. We can't rule over them any more with a rod of iron. Those good old days are dead. Your arrogance stops you from seeing reality but I bet you are aware of it. You have tried to run the whole show but you know very well that the time has come to change your methods."

"Enough, enough," they said, banging on the table with their fists.

"The meeting is over," said the chairman. "You, Pierre, can pack your bags. "Your stay here has poisoned your mind and you need some rest. Go on leave."

"What!... but I'm delighted. I've been able to get that off my chest. I've been asking for ages to be repatriated. Every time I've been refused!"

There was silence. Then one by one they dispersed in the club, mixing with other groups.

Everything that had happened in the meeting that evening was common knowledge the next day in every neighbourhood in the town.

Chapter 4

"Papa" Gomis, as he had been nicknamed by the young friends out of respect for his age and also because of his easy-going nature, had agreed to meet Oumar that evening on the quay. In fact he had the habit when his day's work ended to go for a stroll on the wharf to think back over the events of the day and reflect a little about his life.

Papa Gomis had brought up his three sons as Christians and it had given him great joy that the eldest had taken Holy Orders. The youngest son was studying in Dakar; as for Jean, he preferred to stay in the fold and help his father in the shop.

Up to then the life of the family had carried on smoothly. In good years and bad the business brought in enough to feed everyone and for the rest they accepted whatever life would offer them. Due to the education provided by the missionaries he habitually entrusted himself to Providence and otherwise the peaceful and successful life he had led for around thirty years seemed unlikely to provoke any serious upsets. Nonetheless he also had his dreams. When he first arrived in Ziguinchor, there was no shop apart from his own. At the present time he was still the only black shopkeeper – from which he drew a certain pride – but the businesses run by the Whites had prospered more quickly and more thoroughly than his.

In addition, Gomis had allowed himself to be attracted by Oumar Faye's projects. The boldness of the young man clashed with his own faintheartedness, but at the same time they attracted him. How, when he had only been here for two growing seasons people were saying that half of the next season's harvest would be sold to him? Was it really true that times were changing and that his own son could overcome the apprehensions and fears he had felt throughout his life?

Sitting on the edge of the wharf with his legs dangling above the water, Gomis was gazing but not seeing the huge river which was beginning to fade into the darkness. The sound of men and women laughing and the prying beam of an electric torch shook him from his reverie. Oumar and Isabelle, then Desiree followed by Agbo, and Seck in the rear, were coming towards him. He heard the cheerful voice of Faye saying: "And now my children, the joking is over, and we have to talk about serious matters."

They all settled down around the old shopkeeper, some seated, others lying down. Isabelle stretched herself full length on the wooden planks with her head resting on her husband's lap. There was a long silence which Gomis was the first to break, saying: "Your wife is very brave, Oumar. When do you expect the baby to be due?"

"At the right time in the hot season and I'm thinking of inviting her sister to come from France."

"For the baptism?" interrupted papa Gomis. "Is she a Christian? Will you baptise the child in the church?"

"I don't think so. At least we have not yet discussed it."

"So the child will be a Muslim?"

"No again. The child will have the name that we give. As for faith, that's a matter for when he or she reaches the age of consent."

"That's a good principle," Seck commented.

But Papa Gomis did not share this opinion: "My children, faith is necessary. It guides us. A society without religious education is nothing but a society of animals."

There was another silence and the elderly shopkeeper understood that the gulf which separated the generations was not only about farming methods or business principles.

It was Faye's turn to break the silence. His voice had taken on a more serious tone: "Papa Gomis, I have not come here to ask if it is better to be a Muslim, a Christian or a fetishist. I want to create a model farm from which everyone will profit and I have come to see if you would like to associate with me. It is important that someone capable runs the business side. I first thought of my uncle but he didn't understand that I wanted to go with him in that direction. Before coming to see you I talked with Jean. He agrees. We are going to try to create an agricultural co-operative with a sales office which would respond to the farmers' needs and support their interests. The price per hundredweight must no longer be imposed on us; we must be able to discuss it. Next year I shall have two ploughs and after that it will be time for a tractor. As you know, it is the custom among our people that the elders take the lead. You have had your time; you must do more than just be a spectator now our time has come."

"I'm greatly flattered," said Papa Gomis whose voice was trembling slightly, "but we have to think carefully. Those who surround us have long arms. If I have understood well you want to compete with the big traders?"

It was Agbo who interrupted: "No, Papa Gomis, you should not misinterpret Faye's words. He has simply found, and I agree with him, that it would be good to bring together all the farmers to be able to deal with the big traders as you say. Casamance is the granary of Senegal. Everyone must be able to profit from it."

Seck intervened in turn in the rather pompous tone he used when he was giving schoolchildren a lesson in morality: "Papa Gomis, forgive me for what I am about to say for there is another thing that you must understand. My father, Faye's father, you and a number of others, you did not come here because you loved palm trees. When you left your villages for the shores of the Casamance River you came to make your fortune. In those days Faye's father had twenty-five pirogues. The young people were proud of your shop. Kids like us were proud of you. Now there has been progress and it's not you who have profited from it. Your shop is often half empty since the items that you alone used to sell can be found elsewhere, better quality and cheaper. Faye's father no longer has a monopoly of fishing. My own father is entrenched in his pride, trying to be a man of the old school. Are you going to be like the nomadic farmers who go searching for new land to farm? It's not by distancing yourselves from it that you can find the solution to the problem. We should go for it. The trading companies may not be as strong as you think. They are waiting. You want to approach the peasant farmers. I think Faye's proposal comes at the right moment."

Oumar had paid full attention to the teacher. He heard his own words expressed in this level-headed voice and this pleased him.

"Everything you say is wonderful," said Papa Gomis, stooping slightly. "I will give you my response very shortly, when I have spoken to Jean. You're not in hurry, Faye?"

"I'm not, but the rain doesn't wait!"

An owl flew through the night sky flapping heavily. The old man stood up: "Today is Thursday. I'll come to see you on Sunday evening. And for now I wish you good night, my children."

The silhouette of the good-natured old man faded as he moved towards the town.

"Do you think we have thrown him in the deep end?" asked Agbo.

Seck said: "I think he was impressed but that does not tell us anything. I've no idea how he'll respond."

"The man is paralysed by fear and only a major event will make him decide." Isabelle had spoken as she got up to go.

"I think he was moved by Seck's words but I think you've got it right," said Oumar taking his wife's hand.

Chapter 5

Isabelle and Oumar were playing draughts in their bedroom. Outside it was raining and the rhythm of the raindrops on the zinc roof beat out an irritating little song. Faye was not concentrating. He was worried because someone had been talking too much and for the past two days the whole country was talking about his co-operative project.

Faye knew his countrymen. He knew that even at this very moment thousands of people's imaginations were at work and he could not stop anyone sharing this dream of his. The images that his fellow men and women were seeing he had seen many times; he was seeing them again that evening: noisy tractors hauling ploughs across the land from morning till night; all around, the crowd of those not yet initiated looking on longingly. The boldest ones would come forward, calculating the amount of work that could be accomplished by one man in one day and be astonished. When the driver turned at the end of the furrow, the sharp point of the ploughshare would appear and this cutting blade, gleaming and polished by the earth would fascinate them as if it was a miracle. Watching the young men work it looked as though they wanted to damage the land, to punish it. Already no land would be left fallow and the small earth ridges that separated the plots would have disappeared. Within three days three fields would have been ploughed and seeds sown.

And when it was time for a break everyone would come

together again. They would kneel down in front of the hot, shiny ploughshare. They would measure its dimensions comparing it with their primitive, ill-assorted tools. Or they would pick up a handful of steaming earth, knead it between their fingers and hold it up to their face, for it would seem to have for them the warmth and softness of a virgin's cheeks. Bit by bit the machine would win the hearts of the most reluctant ones. The marshes would have been drained, the rice paddies irrigated, miles and miles of bush cleared and the ponds filled with soil. At harvest time in the evenings, before singing and dancing, they would decorate the machine with a sheaf of rice, for those who have helped you during the hard work of the day must never be forgotten …

Faye covered his eyes with his hands: he murmured as though to himself: "It's too soon. Who is the bastard that spilt the beans?"

"Hey, my love, are you dreaming? It's your turn to play," said Isabelle.

Oumar looked in vain for a possible move. The counters he had left were blocked in all directions.

"I think I've lost again," he said.

"Exactly, and here is your bill since the beginning of the year," said Isabelle opening a crumpled piece of paper, "You owe me 27,885 francs."

"One, I'm skint, and two you're a cheat!"

"You only needed to watch me. Right, tomorrow I'll give you double or quits."

"27,885 francs," Oumar repeated as he undressed. "You will end up making me lose everything, including my wife!"

"Your wife, I don't want her with that belly on her, thanks!"

"That's a shame. I could have let her go for half price," Oumar added, pinching Isabelle's ear.

Then he turned down the wick on the lamp and opened out the mosquito net. Tired out, lulled by the rain on the roof and assisted by the silence, Oumar quickly fell asleep.

"Tomorrow I would like to go to church," said Isabelle.

"Huh, what?"

"Yes, Desiree wants to take me there."

"Well, as you wish …. What is that?…"

A moment earlier it seemed to them that there were cries in the distance. Now there was no room for doubt. Someone out there was crying for help.

"Who could be crying like that?" asked Oumar. "Can you hear it too?"

They listened again, thinking of nothing but the cries.

"It's true," said Isabelle, "Someone is calling but who can it be in this downpour?"

"Perhaps someone collecting gourds who has lost their balance. Last week somebody stole some *dolo* gourds."

The cries grew more urgent. It was impossible to sleep. Faye got out of bed: "I'm going to see. Perhaps there was a landslide just as someone was passing by."

"Possible. Your raincoat is downstairs and your boots are in the kitchen."

"Oh well, with three women in the house I am well looked after. It's well worth the 27,000 plus whatever …"

"27,885 francs," said Isabelle.

Faye had put on his bath robe. Downstairs he found Itylima opening her eyes wide, a lamp in her hand. He took it and put it on the pedestal.

"Are you afraid? Of what?"

"He's been shouting for a long time. Then I heard some footsteps…," she said, hitching up her wrapper.

"Go back to bed," he ordered her as he got dressed. "But where is my mother?"

"I'm here," said Rokhaya who was in the next room. "I heard steps and howls. It sounds as if someone was wounded."

Oumar spoke in French: "For once your wisdom is powerless."

"I didn't understand what you just said"

Oumar came back from the kitchen with his boots on. "I wasn't speaking to you."

He shut the door behind him. The night was as dark as the depth of an abyss. With the aid of his electric flashlight he avoided the puddles. Once outside his own land he let himself be guided by the shouts. 'I must install a lamp here at the lookout,' he thought. The drops of rain like crystal threads crossed the beam of light. Faye went from tree to tree, ever deeper into the woods. He reached the stream but could see nothing. The shouts came from his left. He diverted, crossed the lookout post and stopped to listen. He could hear nothing apart from the rain beating down and the sound of a few creatures disturbed from their sleep.

"Don't be frightened, I'm not the landlord," he cried in the hope that some response would lead him to the source of the sound. But there was no response.

'Damn it, but yet I'm not mad,' he said to himself.

He took a few more steps, pointing his lamp towards the south. There was nothing but palm trees there. He turned back. From one second to the next he stopped still, shining the beam of his light on the tree trunks and the bushes, then he walked ahead on the waterlogged ground.

He had spent a good half-hour inspecting the bushes. Convinced that he had got it wrong he got ready to return. Suddenly, from behind him someone gave him a blow on the head. As soon as he was recovering from that another blow landed on his shoulder. He wanted to stand up to the attack but the blows intensified, coming from both sides at the same time. He had the strength to rally and he grabbed one of the assailants. He forced both his knees on to the ground and was still holding on. He heard a voice saying: "He's holding me! Attack his arm!"

The violence of the blow gave Faye the impression that his right forearm was broken. He collapsed and lay on the grass face downwards. With a last convulsive movement he tried to lift his arms again. Then they kicked him roughly, stamped on him and abandoned him.

Faye crawled towards the stream. His head ached badly, his body was a mass of pain. With his throat and his mouth full of blood he was even incapable of uttering any sound. For a moment more he dragged himself along …

Meanwhile at La Palmeraie Isabelle had gone back to bed. But seeing that her husband had not returned she got up and went to wake Rokhaya and Itylima. The three women looked in each other's eyes. They heard no further sound outside. Isabelle said, "I'm going to go and see. It's not normal for him to take such a long time. It's over an hour since he left."

The old woman held her hand and said: "You malatte … much water … me go."

Before going out she went back to her room, loaded her Tyrolean pipe and lit it. Isabelle dressed her in her beige linen cape, but she refused to wear shoes. Sick at heart, the young woman watched Rokhaya go towards the stream with the hurricane lamp in her hand.

Chapter 6

It was a Sunday morning. The air smelt fresh after a night of rain. The atmosphere was calm and tranquil.

The church square was crowded with the faithful who were pouring out of the church, each one clutching a prayer book. Their costumes varied greatly: some were entwined in wrappers; others were wearing brightly coloured suits. The women, who were in the majority, wore long dresses of printed cloth and the elderly ladies had robes reaching to their ankles. They had a predilection for black satin that caught the reflection of the sunshine as if it was a coat of armour. Their white hair was hidden under tied head-scarves. Children sensibly held hands with grown-ups but pulled faces at each other as they passed.

A large number of parishioners were moving towards the small market place to chat. They would talk together about a thousand unimportant things. They would exchange recipes, get news of the newest born babies, chatter about a girl who when night came went back out to her boyfriend. The small market place was the favourite spot for scandal.

The Gomis had a large following. The head of the family, as stiff as his starched collar, had at his side his wife in a long dress. John and Agnes followed. The girl was wearing a light blue crêpe de chine dress. She was talking excitedly to Jean: "Seck pushed your dad hard last night, you know. Faye only had to shake him a bit. Do you think he will accept?"

"No," Jean Gomis replied, "This morning he told me he

was an old man, that what Seck said was true … but that he preferred his steady life."

"But … what about you?"

"Me? Oh, I obey. My mother spent the whole night preaching to me."

"Ah!" gasped Agnes.

Desiree caught up with them. Her shock of hair fluttered behind her like the mane of a thoroughbred. She was walking nimbly with her wide skirt allowing her strong legs plenty of room to move.

"Hey, where are you rushing?" asked Jean Gomis.

"You are too inquisitive .… Hi Agnes!"

At that moment they saw Agbo coming to meet them with heavy drops of sweat on his brow. He stopped in front of Papa Gomis and whispered in his ear. Total shock was reflected in the shopkeeper's face. The doctor then spoke to the group of young people.

"Faye was killed last night," he told them.

"You're lying!" Desiree blurted out uncontrollably, feverishly holding her fingers to her mouth.

"It's tragic, for sure, but it's the truth. He breathed his last in my arms," added the doctor.

The sermon was no longer the main item of gossip. The news of Faye's death spread rapidly by word of mouth. The most respectable church members surrounded Papa Gomis. Suddenly every face bore a mask of sadness. People wondered: "What did he die of?" Remembering that he was still there the evening before, they just could not believe it.

The doctor continued: "It was just after the rain stopped. The maid, little Itylima, came looking for me. She said that Faye was wounded. I rushed to La Palmeraie. Maman Rokhaya and Isabelle were crying their eyes out. I saw

Oumar lying on the couch in the sitting room with quantities of blood flowing from his mouth. Impossible to make him speak. He was already more dead than alive.... His mother explained what had happened in the night. She had found him lying flat in the mud. We don't know how many guys threw themselves at him. And the most appalling thing was that he had gone out to help someone, as they had heard groans that seemed to come from a wounded person .... Then they literally massacred him.

In small groups they made their way to La Palmeraie.

Drums were sounding. The rhythm of its beat became more and more fitful, more and more bewitching. Their sound crossed the land, leaping to the far side of the river where a similar rhythm took over, sending every person the echoes of the message of bereavement.

Like a rising tide, people arrived at La Palmeraie, some by boat, some on foot. The house was packed full and the crowd stretched to the edge of the stream. They pointed out to each other the very spot where Rokhaya had found the body. She had dragged it as far as the entrance to the house. The people walked silently behind her, trying not to destroy the evidence of her agonising effort. From time to time someone in the crowd would repeat the question for the third or the fifth time: "Why did they kill him?", or they asked, knowing already that there would be no answer: "Who are the murderers?" They satisfied themselves with the favour of a look which meant: "Oh Brother, we know nothing. Shall we know, perhaps, before we leave this place?"

And the voice of the drum was still rumbling, calling the living and providing an accompaniment to death.

All those living along the river were there, from the source of the Casamance to the edge of the bush. The Mandinka had come, and the Aparides, even people from the land of the Nipningues. The pulse of the city had stopped beating. It was overcome with a huge sadness.

After the burial, everyone, Christians, Muslims, fetishists, pagans and atheists, gathered and returned to La Palmeraie. Seck, Agbo, Jean Gomis and Diagne had carried their comrade on their shoulders. Isabelle, in black, walked between Desiree and Agnes. Papa and Mama Gomis led the human flood walking behind.

Isabelle entered the house. Rokhaya, together with some other elderly women and helped by Seynabou and Itylima, looked after the visitors.

"I think this is not the moment to talk about … things," said the old shopkeeper who had accompanied Isabelle.

"No, Papa Gomis."

She had large blueish shadows under her eyes. Her lips quivered with suffering. They were indoors in the sitting room while, outside, people were waiting.

She went on: "It's his actions you wanted to talk about, I think it's up to you to take a decision. I have not lived for a very long time with him, alas. But I know what I would prefer if I were in his place. I would want to continue what I had started. This was his country, these people were his raison d'être. He loved France very much but he preferred Africa. I am only one of you by virtue of our marriage and the child I am bearing … maybe he also will be one of you. If you want me to say something, Papa Gomis, don't be angry. My grief is my own but the land where his body rests is yours."

Overcome, Gomis bowed his head, waited a moment in silence and then went out on to the veranda. He looked at the crowd. He had never seen so many people gathered, facing him. He toyed with his gloves. The anxious crowd were all ears. The drum had stopped playing its dirge.

Gomis spoke: "My dear people, I have been asked to give you our thanks." This was the usual formula of African politeness. The old man chose his words carefully.

"Madame Faye thanks you and praises you. She has asked me to speak on her behalf. We are all touched by the sadness which she is experiencing. She would have preferred to say these words to you herself … but she sincerely accepts your condolences …"

Everyone murmured. A few clouds raced low in the sky.

He went on: "Today we have buried one of our own, a son of this country, the brother of some, the cousin of others, a friend, a counsellor, a guide. It is two years since he arrived here with his wife. We thought at that moment that he had disowned his race, that he was no longer one of us …. Well, this was not true. Faye came back to us as though he had never left the country. He showed us, despite his young age, that we are men. He said to my son: "It's not marrying a woman that makes a man a man. To be a man you must struggle hard. You must extract from each thing its secret and make it your own, for the good of everybody …"

He paused to wipe the sweat which was running down his face. Then he continued: "You all know that Faye wanted you to be united. And that is why he was killed. He told me before he was murdered that some among you were aware of this. All of us must unite and be strong. This country is ours, it's the heritage of our ancestors. It is up to us to take it back from those who want to snatch it from us. For do you remember these words: 'The king may take your sons to make war far away, your wife will permit it; if he takes away your herds in time you may forget it, but if he takes your land that means he wants to kill you … and the one who wants your death does not care about your suffering.'"

Gomis finished. He knew he had no more to say. He turned round and looked for a rapid way to depart. He saw Isabelle and clasped her hands in his.

In the evening the drums were still beating. Rokhaya, mad with grief, clung to her daughter-in-law. There was a big family meeting. Uncle Amadou acted as interpreter as well as he could.

"Madame ptetre go home, papa, mama, France…?"

For the white woman this was the most heart-rending moment. Her mother-in-law was at her side, weeping. The uncle carried on, doing his best to make himself understood. "Maman Rokhaya … happy you stay till get baby. Faye, Maman Rokhaya son dead. You, Madame Faye, baby for you, grandson for Maman Rokhaya."

Isabelle was distraught. Were they not asking her too much? The old lady clasped her hands and spoke again: "Madame, stay, get baby," wanting to say that she should stay until she gave birth.

With tears in her eyes and her heart overloaded with grief, Isabelle bowed her head as a sign of acquiescence.

"Merci 'Madame', you zentille femme."

Nothing more was required. Isabelle climbed, sobbing, to her bedroom.

Oumar Faye was dead and buried in the ground. But the criminals who had destroyed him had deluded themselves. The tomb was not his dwelling place but the hearts of every man and every woman. His presence was felt each evening in every home and each day in the rice fields. When a child cried, the mother would recount the story of the young man who talked to the land. And in the shade of the palaver tree they would honour his memory. Oumar was no more, but his 'beautiful people' sang of him always in the sowing season. He heralded the sowing of the seeds, was there during the rainy season and accompanied the young farmers during the harvest.

Glossary

alpenstock (Fr.): Long metal-tipped walking stick.

assalamalec: Short form of 'as salaam alaikum', peace be unto you.

banco: yellow mud and chopped straw used as building material.

boubou: long gown, partly open at sides.

brancou: Creole for a white woman.

busulu: Joola wrestling technique to bring opponents to their knees.

caïlcédrat: Senegalese mahogany tree (khaya senegalensis).

canari: clay jar used to carry and store water.

candabe: belt of palm branches used by palm-wine tappers.

Cangourang: Spirit in human form living in the bush and capable of superhuman efforts.

chicotte: long knotted leather whip with a wooden handle.

conco: hoe.

Croix de Guerre (Fr.): French military decoration for bravery.

daara: koranic school.

damels: ancient kings of Senegal.

dempéting: harvested rice, dried in the sun to preserve.

dolo: gourd used for carrying beer.

dramba: rice farming tool.

*faya*l: large pirogue.

Firandou: great Joola fetishist.

gardes-cercle (Fr.): district police.

griot: historian, storyteller, praise singer, poet, and musician.

gueule: wooden plate.

hames: sorcerer's vessel in a fetishist's hut or sacred place.

imam: leader of prayer in a mosque.

insh'Allah: (Ar.) if God wills it, or God-willing.

jàam rekk: literally peace only meaning well, okay.

kaay: come.

kadiando: rice farming tool.

kinkilibaa/quinquiliba: herbal tea.

korité: Islamic feast of Eid al-Fitr.

kuco: rice farming tool.

laqad jaakum: verse from Koran cited by Muslims to shield them from enemy bullets.

légos: type of imported cloth named after Lagos.

marraine de guerre: war 'godmother' – woman volunteer helping soldiers unsupported by family.

m'balou: begging bowl.

minnediérou brancou: white woman.

muezzin: singer of the call to prayer in Islam.

oboles: alms for a dead person.

pagne: cloth body wrap.

n'iangkalang: boiled rice.

pirogue: narrow wooden canoe boat for transport and fishing.

poto-poto: see banco.

sabador: kaftan.

taibas: tailored blouse jacket.

tiavali: white cloth dyed with indigo.

toubaab: white person.

Tugal/Tougueul: France.

yaay: mother.

yoss: fibre from a shrub dyed black for use as a wig.

Bibliography and Filmography

Books

Le Docker Noir (novel) – Paris: Debresse, 1956; translated as *Black Docker*, London: Heinemann, 1987.

Ô Pays, Mon Beau Peuple! (novel) – Paris: Le Livre Contemporain/ Amiot-Dumont, 1957; translated as *Oh My Country, My Beautiful People!*, London: Books of Africa, 2024.

Les Bouts de Bois de Dieu (novel) – Paris: Le Livre Contemporain/ Amiot Dumont, 1960; translated as *God's Bits of Wood*, London: Heinemann, 1970.
Voltaïque (short stories) – Paris: Présence Africaine, 1962; translated as *Tribal Scars*, London: Heinemann, 1974.

L'Harmattan (novel) – Paris: Présence Africaine, 1964.

Le Mandat, précédé de Vehi-Ciosane (short stories) – Paris: Présence Africaine, 1966; translated as *The Money-Order with White Genesis*, London: Heinemann, 1987.

Xala (novel) – Paris: Présence Africaine, 1973; translated as *Xala*, London: Heinemann, 1976.

Le Dernier de l'Empire (novel) – Paris, L'Harmattan, 1981; translated as *The Last of the Empire*, London: Heinemann, 1983.

Niiwam (short stories) – Paris: Présence Africaine, 1987; translated as *Niiwam and Taaw: Two Novellas*, London: Heinemann, 1992.

Films

Borom Sarret (1963)
Niaye (1964)
La Noire de... (1966)
Mandabi (1968)
Emitaï (1971)
Xala (1975)
Ceddo (1977)
Camp de Thiaroye (1988)
Guelwaar (1992)
Faat Kiné (2000)
Moolaadé (2004)